WALK TALL,
RIDE TALL

by BURT and BUDD ARTHUR

A SIGNET BOOK from
NEW AMERICAN LIBRARY
TIMES MIRROR

SIGNET TRADEMARK REG. U.S. PAT. OFF. AND FOREIGN COUNTRIES
REGISTERED TRADEMARK—MARCA REGISTRADA
HECHO EN CHICAGO, U.S.A.

SIGNET, SIGNET CLASSICS, SIGNETTE, MENTOR AND PLUME BOOKS
are published by The New American Library, Inc.,
1301 Avenue of the Americas, New York, New York 10019

FIRST PRINTING, AUGUST, 1965

PRINTED IN THE UNITED STATES OF AMERICA

ONE

In the summertime when the heat lay heavily over the rangeland and the wilting sun put a stop to all outdoor activity in the tiny cattle towns that dotted it, Ossie Blue's saloon in Indian Head was the most comfortable spot in town. A cool breeze that whipped up quite mysteriously in Blue's cluttered back yard danced into the saloon through the wide open back door. It played over the bar and made standing there a delight for Ossie's customers; broadening its sweep, it spanned the place from wall to wall so that table-sitters were able to enjoy the breeze too. Ossie was not the kind to look a gift horse in the mouth. So he made no attempt to figure out why he alone of the three saloonkeepers in Indian Head should be so blessed; a blessing, he maintained, should be enjoyed and should not be questioned. So, much to the resentment of his competitors, he did a land-office business and welcomed each year's arrival of summer with understandable glee.

But this year things were different. Summer came on schedule and brought with it the usual oppressive heat. The cooling breeze came prancing in just as it had every year before. It should have brought the expected stream of sweltering townsmen crowding into Ossie's, eager to be revived by the breeze. The fact that it hadn't caused him great concern. It wasn't because he couldn't explain his failure to do his usual summertime business. He could. But what irked him was the realization that he couldn't do anything about it. As he whisked his rag over the bar's glistening surface, an unnecessary gesture since there hadn't been any customers in the place in two days, his gaze lifted and focused upon three youths who were idling just inside the open front door. The trio had taken to hanging out in Ossie's saloon, and their antics and horseplay had proved so annoying to his customers that they had simply taken themselves and their thirst elsewhere. A mixture of frustration and rage welled up inside of Ossie and showed in his normally mild eyes. A slightly built man of about forty-seven, of some one hundred and twenty pounds in weight and about five feet two inches tall, Ossie had already conceded that he was physically powerless to oust the unwanted trio, and that someone else would have to do it for him.

As he continued to eye the back-turned youths, he thought bitterly to himself: "Young squirts, they aren't dry yet behind the ears. But each one's packin' a gun and looking for trouble. Each thinks he's just about the fastest gun around and is looking for a chance to prove it. Years ago there were a couple o' men around here who were right handy with a gun. They woulda taken on any one o' those squirts, maybe even all three of them at the same time, and they woulda fixed them good. Some o' those men are still around. But they're older now, and the years have done something to them same's it's done to everybody else. They don't make the quick moves that they used to, their hands aren't as steady and their eyes have taken to playing tricks on them. So they don't see 'ny point in taking on something they aren't up to handling and winding up getting th'mselves gunned down by some punk kid. So they steer clear o' them, and they're willing to leave it to somebody else, somebody who's up to doing the job that they wouldn't have waited to be asked to do when they were younger. Wish to hell these three would get tired of waiting and take each other on. Maybe then with some luck they'd kill each other off and I'd be damned will rid of them."

But much to Ossie's disappointment, they seemed to get along well with one another. So in desperation the saloonkeeper had to humble himself.

"Ah, look, fellers, give me a chance, willya, and go hang out somewhere's else?" he pleaded with them. "Another couple o' days like the last two with nobody willing to come in here and put up with the way you fellers plague th'm, and I'll have to close up. That what you want to see happen? Must be, even though I can't figure out why, being that I've never done anything to any of you. So how about it?"

"You've got this all wrong, Ossie," answered Paulie Voight, a good-looking, trimly built, dark-complexioned youth of about twenty, and the leader of the trio. "We aren't keeping people from coming in here. Oh-h, I admit we like to have some fun. But you know same's I do that this town's dying on its feet, and to keep it alive it needs livening up. That's all we do.

6

Liven things up a bit. So you're way off when you go pickin' on us for what's happened. I think it must be you, Ossie, something about you, or something you do, or maybe it's the beer you've been serving up lately that's soured people on you so that they've taken to going somewhere's else."

"I think it's the beer," added one of Paulie's companions, the youngest of the trio, a blond, almost baby-faced boy of eighteen named Tommy Thayer. "Seemed to me it was kinda flat last night. Didn't want to say anything before. But now that Paulie's mentioned it . . ."

"There y'are, Ossie," Paulie said, interrupting young Thayer. "There's the answer to it." But then his lips tightened. "I don't like it when somebody takes to blaming us for something that isn't any of our doing."

His right hand dropped and curled around the butt of his gun. The significance of it was not lost upon Ossie. He said no more, averted his eyes, and plied his rag more vigorously.

"If we had a sheriff in this lousy hole of a town who wasn't a-scared of his own shadow," he was thinking to himself, and as bitterly as before, "he'd chase those three young hellions outta here and he'd see to it that they stayed out too. Then decent people could come in here again like they used to, to enjoy a cold glass of beer while the breeze refreshed th'm. Ain't up to me to do the chasin' out. Up to the law. That's what we pay him for. No point though in expecting Ab Peaseley to do anything. He hasn't got the guts." After a moment-long pause: "Oh-h, if only somebody who wasn't a-scared o' them would come in and fix them good when they start their foolin' around and . . ."

He had raised his head the barest bit. He stole an almost guarded look at the three youths. Unconsciously he stopped his wiping down and he stared a little. A tall man whom he knew he had never seen before was standing on the walk outside; as Ossie stared at him, the man hunched his broad shoulders and bent his head so that he might see inside, then suddenly straightened up and came striding in. Ossie caught and held his breath, gulped, and swallowed hard when the stranger shouldered his way through the three, who made no attempt to step aside so that he might pass. As he headed directly for the bar, the trio wheeled around after him, and Ossie felt a queasy, sinking feeling in the pit of his stomach. The man nodded to him as he came up to the bar and leaned over it, resting his forearms on its curved lip.

"Beer," he said, thumbing his hat up from his forehead, revealing a shock of bright red hair. "And I hope it's cold."

"It's cold all right, mister," Ossie answered him, and he paled as the three youths neared the bar.

7

Paulie swerved away from his companions to take up his position on the tall man's right while Thayer and the third boy, Curly Simmons, who was a little older than Thayer, came up to the bar on the man's left.

"Now look, boys," Ossie began nervously, sensing that there was going to be trouble, "it's too hot today for any foolin' around. So don't start any and leave this man be."

"Why, Ossie, I'm surprised at you," Paulie said in feigned hurt tones. "Man's a stranger here, and being that we're the friendly and hospitable kind, and nobody knows that better than you, we aim to make him feel at home. Even though the way he pushed in on us wasn't exactly friendly. But like you said, it's a hot day, and the heat's liable to make a man forget his manners. So we're willing to forgive and forget. All right, Ossie?"

"We-ll . . ."

Drawing back a bit from the tall man and eyeing the latter's low-slung gun, Paulie said: "That big 'C' in the heel plate, Mac. What's it stand for?"

"My name," was the reply.

"No foolin'? For your name, huh? We-ll, what d'you know? So what's the name it stands for?"

"Canavan."

"It supposed to mean something to me?"

"No more, I don't suppose, than yours would to me."

"Mine'll mean a helluva lot one o' these days."

"How about that beer?" Canavan asked Ossie.

"Wear your gun low," Paulie commented, "like a regular gun thrower." Then moving a step closer to Canavan, he said with a shake of his head: "That's bad, Mac. That's looking for trouble. Somebody who doesn't like hired guns and thinks you might be one, or who's looking to take on somebody who thinks he's a fast gun to show him he isn't, might—"

"I'm telling you to cut it out, Paulie," Ossie interrupted him as he set a foaming glass of beer on the bar squarely in front of Canavan. "I said, leave him be."

Suddenly Thayer, who was standing next to the tall man, reached out and the glass of beer went slithering down the bar. Its flight ended abruptly when Curly Simmons' hand shot out, halting it. In almost the same deft motion Curly brought it closer to him, imprisoning it within the laced fingers of his two hands. Thayer and he grinned at each other.

Paulie's reaction was a cross between a light laugh and a chuckle. "Those two partners of mine've got the fastest hands you'll ever see," he said to Canavan. Then addressing himself to Ossie: "Curly isn't the kind that likes to drink alone, and I don't think our friend here would like it if Tommy and me

8

didn't drink with him. So c'mon, Ossie. Three more beers."

The saloonkeeper frowned. But wisely, simply because he knew he had no means of stopping the trio, he held his tongue, and placed three more glasses of beer on the bar. He pushed the middle one into Canavan's waiting hands. Thayer reached for the glass nearest him while Paulie took the remaining one. Canavan raised his glass to his lips and drank some of his beer, put it down, dug in his pocket, produced a coin and slapped it on the bar.

Paulie looked at it, put down his glass, and said evenly: "That isn't enough, Mac."

When Canavan, ignoring him, sought to lift his glass again, Paulie put his hand on Canavan's right wrist, stopping him.

"I said that isn't enough, Mac."

"I only ordered one beer," Canavan answered quietly, "and that's what I paid for."

Paulie smiled thinly and said: "Man's waiting for thirty cents more."

"He isn't getting it from me."

"I think you'd better pay him, Mac."

Ossie's fear-filled eyes shuttled back and forth between them. Now his gaze halted and held on Canavan, who was silent and motionless. Then with a startlingly sudden and obviously unexpected twist of his wrist that freed it of Paulie's restraining hand, Canavan flung the contents of his glass squarely into Paulie's face. A gasp that Ossie could not stifle burst from him. Half-turning, Canavan cuffed Thayer viciously in the face with the back of his big left hand. Paulie cursed, and Thayer, careening backward, trampled Simmons, bumped him too, causing him to overturn his glass and douse himself with his beer. Wide-eyed and open-mouthed, Ossie saw Paulie, with his face dripping and beer beading his nose, claw for his gun. He caught a glimpse of Canavan backing off from the bar. As Paulie's gun cleared the lip of his holster and he jerked it upward, there was a roar of gunfire. Canavan's bullet, fired at practically point-blank range, slammed into Paulie with such force that it flung him around. Ossie saw him drop his gun and stumble blindly along the bar. Clinging to it with his left hand, Paulie sank to his knees and hung from it with his head bowed.

Another clap of thunder, this one surprisingly enough louder than the first, rocked the saloon, made the stacks of upended glasses on the towel-covered shelves on the back wall tinkle, and made Ossie wince and blink his eyes. He heard someone cry out. Instinctively he turned his head. It was Tommy Thayer whose cry he had heard. Clutching his right wrist to him with his left hand, the youth was rocking and moaning. When he raised his head for a brief moment, Ossie saw that as a result of Canavan's backhanded blow, blood was bubbling in his battered nostrils and there was a thin smear of it on his lips. Blood was spouting from Thayer's right wrist, and it was drenching both of his hands. Some of it burst through his fingers and ran down his pants' leg and onto his boots. Ossie, following the course of the dripping blood with his eyes, spotted a gun lying on the floor between Thayer's feet.

Raising his gaze again, Ossie glimpsed someone else who was standing diagonally behind Thayer. It was Curly Simmons, and he stood with his empty hands raised as Canavan's fire-blackened gun muzzle gaped at him. His shirt front was beer-wet and clung to his body. His face was so white, it looked ghostlike. Ossie noticed that his gun was still holstered. Idly he wondered if the youth had sought to draw it only to be cowed when Canavan leveled his gun at him, or if he had made no attempt to yank it out when he saw what had happened to his companions.

Both Ossie and Canavan were suddenly aware of an audience of wide-eyed men who were crowded into the open doorway and who were staring in.

"Don't all of you just stand there, you danged fools!" Ossie yelled at them. "Somebody go fetch Doc Anderson. Tell him he's got two customers waiting for him here and to get a hustle on!"

Still holding his gun on Simmons, Canavan backed off even more and collided with a chair that hadn't been pushed in very close to a small table. He reached behind him with his left hand and swung it around. Settling it in front of him, he straddled it with the barrel of his gun leveled across the top of the chair's back rest, and waited.

"All right, all right now," Canavan heard a man say authoritatively. "Lemme through." He stole a quick look in the direction of the crowded doorway. A medium-sized, middle-aged, bespectacled man pushed into the saloon. He wore a badly tarnished star pinned to his unbuttoned and loosely hanging vest, a holstered gun that rode high on his hip, and a hat that had seen better days. The lawman slowed his step when he neared Thayer and Simmons, stopped when he came abreast of them, and eyed them frowningly. When he gestured, the Simmons boy lowered his arms and let them hang limply at his sides. The man sauntered on, glanced at Canavan, passed him, and halted when he came to where Paulie Voight, still on his knees and still head-bent, lay slumped against the bar.

He looked down at the hapless youth, slowly straightened

10

up, and came trudging back. "You, mister," he said to Canavan, flicking his right hand at him. "You do this?"

"Damned right he did," Ossie said before Canavan could answer. "And he had every right to. Those three punk kids have been bedeviling—"

"I didn't ask you," the sheriff said curtly over his rounded shoulder to Ossie. "I asked him. So supposing you let him answer?"

Freed of his fear of the troublesome trio, Ossie's pent-up frustration and rage refused to remain stifled any longer and burst from him completely out of control.

"If we had a sheriff here instead of a pussyfootin' old goat who couldn't make a go of storekeeping and who hasn't done 'ny better upholding the law," he yelled at the lawman, his face flaming, "this wouldn't've happened!"

The sheriff squared around to Ossie.

"You'd better shut up, Blue," he said, shaking a crooked finger threateningly at the saloonkeeper. "You run off at the mouth too much. One o' these days when I've had enough of you, I'll run you the hell into a cell, lock you in, and throw away the key and let you rot in there." Ossie held his tongue. His rage having spent itself, and having said his piece, he seemed to be satisfied. The sheriff glowered at him over the tops of his spectacles. When Ossie made no attempt to say anything more, the lawman, mistakingly thinking that he had cowed him into silence, grunted, turned again to Canavan, and gave him a long, hard look. "All right, mister," he said curtly, pushing his metal-rimmed glasses higher up on his nose. "Put your gun away. What's your name, where d'you come from, and what are you doing here in Indian Head?"

Canavan shoved his gun down into his holster, got up, scaled the chair away, and answered simply: "Name's Canavan. I'm from Truxton. I came here—"

"Man your size, a full-growed man too," the sheriff said, interrupting him. "You oughta be ashamed of yourself. Why don't you go pick on somebody your size instead of a couple o' kids who don't mean any harm to anybody?"

"Maybe you oughta see to it that kids aren't allowed in your saloons, and you might make it a point to warn them that if they go looking for trouble, they're bound to find it, and more often than not, a lot more than they can handle," Canavan retorted.

"That's telling 'im, Canavan," Ossie said and he clapped his hands. "That's telling 'im."

Pretending that he hadn't heard Ossie, the sheriff, crimsoning a little under the eyes, said: "We don't like your kind around here, mister. Your kind's trouble. Go get your horse and clear out've here. G'wan now. Get going."

"Just a minute, if you please," a voice that Canavan thought had a somewhat recognizable ring to it said from the crowded doorway. Glancing in its direction, he saw a stocky, white-haired, well-dressed man emerge from the packed ranks of the onlookers and step inside. The man was J. P. Stonebridge, the owner of the Indian Head Bank. He came forward and stopped about midway between Canavan and the sheriff. "Mr. Canavan came here at my invitation," he said to the lawman, "to look over the O-Bar-O. I rode over it with him this morning. Apparently he liked what he saw for he bought it. Indian Head is most fortunate in getting a man of his caliber as one of its citizens. For your further information, Sheriff Peaseley, Mr. Canavan was a Texas Ranger for many years and earned for himself an enviable reputation as a thoroughly competent officer of the law. So in view of what I know about him, I am quite confident that whatever happened here was not of his making, but must have been forced upon him." Turning to Canavan, he said simply: "The papers are ready for your signature. I'll be in my office till five. I'll be expecting you."

His red face reflecting his embarrassment, the sheriff sputtered: "Long's he remembers that I'm the law around here, we'll get along."

Motioning to Curly Simmons, Peaseley herded the youth out of the saloon ahead of him. Stonebridge followed the departing sheriff with his eyes, and shook his head; when Peaseley had gone, the banker gave Canavan a nod, turned on his heel, and headed for the door. A path opened for him and closed behind him only to open again a bare moment or two later to permit still another man to enter. He was a derby-hatted, shirt-sleeved individual who wore sleeve garters, a string bowtie, and suspenders; he carried a small black bag that showed signs of wear and tear.

He stopped abruptly when he came up to Thayer, eyed his bloodied hands, frowned, and shaking his head, muttered, "More of man's inhumanity to man," and walked on. When he came to Paulie Voight, who had slumped forward and who now lay hunched over on his knees with his head touching the floor and his backside higher than the rest of his body, he shook his head again. Putting down his bag, he eased the youth over on his side, bent over him, and after a minute or two straightened up and called: "Couple of you men carry this boy over to my office. And you," he added with a nod to Thayer, "you'd better come along too."

He backed off a couple of steps with his bag in his hand

and watched quietly when four men trudged forward and lifted the unconscious Paulie in their arms. Followed by Thayer, whose contorted face mirrored the pain his shattered wrist was causing him, they carried Paulie out.

The doctor started after them, halted in his tracks, looked back at Canavan, retraced his steps, and said gruffly to him: "There's a passage in the Scriptures that should interest you. It reads: 'He who lives by the sword must surely perish by the sword.' Think that over. Better yet, read it yourself. It may impress you far more than having me quote it to you."

Canavan did not answer. Briskly the doctor walked off and marched out of the saloon.

TWO

Some of the onlookers, the latecomers who had had to stand on tiptoes and crane their necks in order to see what was going on inside the saloon, lost interest once the excitement was over, and backed off and drifted away. Those who remained, probably because they were reluctant to tear themselves away from the breeze that reached out and enveloped them, or because they had nothing better to do with themselves and their time, happily accepted Ossie's invitation to have a nice cold beer on the house. Noisily some seven or eight of them broke out of the doorway and scurried up to the bar, lined up at it, and gleefully collared the foaming glasses that Ossie set before them. Noisily too the beer was gulped down and was followed by a general smacking of lips.

"Doggone it, Ossie," one grizzled old-timer announced as he wiped his mouth with the vein-knotted back of his gnarled hand. "That was just about the best tastin' beer I've had in one helluva long time. Second one on the house too?" he asked with a sly grin.

Ossie, who was feeling pretty much like his old self, grinned back at him.

"Nope," he replied. "Second one's on you."

"Oh-h, so that's the way it is! The freebee was just a come-on, huh?"

Ossie grinned at him again, wordlessly this time. The man produced a silver dollar, eyed it frowningly for a moment, and finally said: "My wife gave me this to buy something with. But I'm damned if I c'n remember what it was. Couldn'ta been anything important though, or I wouldn'ta forgotten it." He slapped the silver piece on the bar. "All right, Ossie.

Played me for a sucker with that come-on. But I'm a willing sucker. So gimme another beer."

"Me too, Ossie," a couple of men chorused together.

"This is still the most comf'table place in town," a man stated flatly. "First time in days that I haven't been wringin' wet with sweat. Hey, Ossie, something just came to me, and I think it's worth hearing."

"Yeah? I'm listening."

"Why don't you take in boarders? I don't mean the kind you have to feed and so on. I mean sleepers. Just give th'm a place to bed down for the night with that nice cool breeze playin' over them, and come morning out they go."

"Hey, wouldn't that be something?"

"And how it would!"

Encouraged by the comments of those around him, the man who had suggested the idea continued with: "Once word got around, you'd have to double the size of this place, Ossie, to take care of the crowd. Say two bits for the use of a sheet or a thin blanket, and, oh-h, maybe ten or fifteen cents tops for a place to lay down, and you'd wind up with enough dough in your kick to buy out old man Stonebridge."

"Lemme think about it," Ossie said as he busied himself refilling the empty foam-ringed glasses that were pushed across the bar at him.

Canavan had found a place for himself apart from the others at the head of the bar, where it right-angled the back wall. No sooner had he leaned over the bar than Ossie brought him a freshly drawn glass of beer.

"What was the doc doing?" Ossie asked him. "Slappin' you with something out've the Bible?"

"Yeah."

"I don't know this for sure, but I have 'n idea he was a preacher before he turned to doctoring."

"Oh?"

"Dunno what happened that made him switch, 'less it was booze that lost him his preaching job," Ossie continued in a confidential tone of voice. "When he first came here I'd find him waiting outside for me to open up and he was the last one outta here when it came closing time. Never saw anybody do a better job of likkerin' himself up than he did. Then all of a sudden he quit the booze. Kinda kept to himself for the longest while after that. Then one day I heard he'd hung out his shingle. There are a lot o' things I'm willing to believe even without seeing th'm. But this wasn't one o' th'm. That boozer a doctor? So I went around to see for myself."

"Hey, Ossie!" one of the men at the bar called and held up his empty glass. "What d'you say?"

15

Ossie didn't say anything. He simply refilled the man's glass and returned to continue his narration, surprising Canavan by picking it up exactly where he had broken it off.

"We-ll, there it was, all right. 'David Anderson, M. D.,' the sign read. He's been doctoring Indian Head ever since, and that must be five, six years by now. From what I've heard tell, he knows his business. At the same time it seems like he's never forgotten the preaching business. He's always sounding off with something from the Bible. Just about everbody in town, men, women, even kids, have had it from him one time or another. So don't you go thinking he was pickin' on you. Far as he's concerned, every last one of us is an out-an'-out sinner, and he never lets us forget it."

There was no response from Canavan. Ossie was silent for a moment or so, then he said musingly: "So you've bought the old Spangler place, huh?"

"That's right."

"Bought yourself something worth owning. That's just about the best piece o' property in the county. Only it isn't gonna make things any easier for you in Indian Head."

"What d'you mean by that?"

"I dunno if you've ever been in a town like this one before . . ."

"Cow towns are usu'lly pretty much alike. They have different names. But everything else about them is us'ully about the same, from the way they're laid out to the kind o' people they have in th'm. So what makes Indian Head stand out from the others?"

" 'Cept for a handful of outsiders like the doc, old man Stonebridge, me, and oh-h, three or four others, all the rest of the Indian Headers are related to each other," Ossie explained.

"All right. But I still don't see—"

"Take that Paulie Voight, the kid you put a slug into. There are more Voights here than any others. Next come the Thayers. The boy whose arm you busted is one o' them. To top it all off the Voights and the Thayers are related to each other too. Now do I have to tell you how you're gonna stand with those people once word gets around that it was you who shot up their kids? They won't wanna know that the kids had it coming to th'm. All they'll wanna know is who did it to th'm."

"I see."

"Now one last thing, partner. You made yourself a helluva good buy when you got the O-Bar-O. Only you're gonna have to watch yourself good because you'll find you've got Voights and Thayers on every side of you."

16

It was about an hour later when Canavan came drumming up the incline that led away from the main road, and reined in about midway between the towering barn and the bunkhouse that faced each other with some thirty or forty feet of smooth, hard-packed ground between them. The doors to the two buildings stood wide open, the one at the top of the ramp that led to it rolled back on its metal trolley, the other pushed back as far as it would go. That morning after Stonebridge had shown him around the place and he had accepted the banker's terms, with the musty smell that had greeted him when he had poked his head inside each still in his nostrils, he had decided that both buildings could do with an airing out. So he had opened the doors wide and had left them that way. The house too was in need of an airing out. But that could wait till he had moved in. Then every window in it as well as the front and back doors would be thrown open wide. Slacking a little in the saddle while his mare stood spread-legged and head-bent and blew herself, Canavan ranged his gaze about him approvingly. He was satisfied that he had made a good buy.

"Old Jake Spangler was what my wife calls a fuss-pot," Stonebridge had told him. "Everything had to be in order and everything in its place. If he wasn't that way before he married, then something of his wife Martha, who was a fine housekeeper, must have rubbed off on him. Even after she died, Jake continued his fussiness. The house, the barn, the bunkhouse—everything was kept in constant repair, and painted regularly. So there shouldn't be anything of any real importance for you to do to ready the place for your wife."

Canavan nudged the mare with his knees and she went on. He glanced mechanically at the corral as they came abreast of it. The bars that formed the enclosure were so smooth-worn they fairly shone.

He drew rein again when he came up to the house, a two-story structure that was painted white, its pushed-back shutters green. The windowpanes gleamed as they caught and reflected the waning afternoon sunlight. Save for some streaks where rain had slanted down and furrowed them, they looked clean. He took particular note of the veranda that fronted the house and ran about halfway around it on both sides. On each side thick-trunked trees whose full branches arched out to rest on the veranda roof shaded it, making it comfortably usable during the day despite the wilting sun. And on summer evenings when cooling breezes drifted over the darkened and hushed range, sitting outside on the veranda would be a delight. He would have to get a couple of chairs suited to that purpose. Rockers, he decided, would be the very thing. In

17

front of the house Elena would doubtless want a garden with a white picket fence around it similar to the one she would be leaving behind her in Truxton. Their new home promised so much, he was getting more and more anxious every minute for her to see it.

Again the mare responded when he nudged her and plodded along the shaded path and rounded the house to the rear. Six sturdy, ramrod-straight poles that needed pulleys and lines to ready them for hanging out wash stood within a dozen or so feet of the back door. Maria, the Mexican woman who served Elena as cook and housekeeper, would find that she had been presented with far more washline room than she had in Truxton.

"And the kitchen she'll be taking over here is just about twice the size o' the one she has now," Canavan told himself. "So she won't be able to complain that she hasn't enough room to work around in."

Suddenly he sat upright, startling the mare, and twisted around, looking surprised and puzzled at the same time. Somewhere beyond him he had heard a grass-muffled rumble of massed hoofs. He wheeled the mare and loped away from the house to a point about a hundred yards from it. He pulled up and leveled a wondering look in the direction from which the thump of hoofbeats had carried.

He hadn't long to wait. A herd of cattle, some two hundred head he judged roughly, came pounding up into view with two horsemen riding the herd's flanks while a third mounted man brought up the rear. They passed him at a distance of probably another hundred yards. Canavan whacked the mare on the rump with the flat of his hand and she bounded away in pursuit of the herd. When Canavan yelled, the man who was riding drag reined in, twisted around, and looked back; when he spotted Canavan coming toward him at a swift run, he swung his horse around, sat back, and waited for Canavan to come up to him.

"Yeah?" he asked as Canavan slowed the mare and pulled up alongside of him. The man's horse eyed the mare interestedly. But when he sought to nuzzle her, she backed off with a curious deep-throated growl that made him retreat and eye her apprehensively. The man astride him grinned. "Damned fool horse'll never learn that he won't get 'nywhere's 'less he takes it easy. He'll get his head kicked off some day and he'll wonder why."

Canavan grunted and said: "This happens to be private property. Mine. Who are you and what are you doing on my land?"

"Name's Brady, Mac. And I'm doing what I was told to

18

do. Fact is, I've been doing it every day for around two years now. Only ord'narily in the morning. Got tied up doing something else this morning, so I had to put it off till around half past two, quarter of three. Me and those other two," and he jerked his head in the direction of the rapidly disappearing herd and the two outriders. "We ride for Had Voight. Right after breakfast we drive the stock down to the stream and water 'em. We're on our way back from there now."

"Only stream I know of around here is about a mile east and it's on my property. That where you've been watering your stock?"

"Uh-huh," Brady acknowledged guiltily. "Only other one's way over west about four miles from our place, and it isn't the easiest place in the world to get to. Ground's rough, hilly in spots and roc'''' *-- And just about every way you turn there are gulleys and ravines that play hell with dumb steers that go piling into th'm hell-bent-for-election and break their spindly legs and sometimes their fool necks and—"

"Sorry, Brady," Canavan said, interrupting him. "But from now on there's where you'll have to do your watering. I don't aim to let your boss, or anybody else for that matter, run their stock over my land. I didn't buy a public road that's open to anybody who wants to use it."

The man nodded understandingly. "I got no argument with that, Mac. If Had wants to argue about it, that's up to him, and between you and him. You won't find him a bad sort. Only he's got a temper that acts up on him every once in a while, and when it does, he hollers. We're used to hearing him sound off, and we know that once he gets the mad out of his system, he isn't the worst kind around. 'Course I figure that when I tell him about this, he'll really do a job of hollering. And what he'll do when he calms down—"

"There isn't anything he can do. So if he wants to holler, let him. It won't get him anywhere."

Brady turned his head. His companions and the herd they were shepherding back to their own place had disappeared completely from sight. Squaring around again, he settled himself in the saddle.

"We-ll," he said to Canavan. "Think I'd better get going. To tell you the truth, there are times when I get a . . . a bang outta hearing Had holler. I kinda think this is gonna be one o' those times. So I wanna get back and hear him explode."

He grinned as he backed his horse and wheeled him.

"So long, Canavan," he called over his shoulder as he rode off.

"So long, Brady," Canavan responded.

He followed the man briefly with his eyes, swung the mare

around, and drummed back to the house, thinking the while to himself: "Hope the stores are still open when I get back to town. I'd head there now only I think I'd better wait around a bit just in case Brady's hollering boss shows up here."

He climbed down from the mare at the back door and went inside. He sauntered about idly from room to room, trudged upstairs too, and continued his sauntering. A little later on when he emerged from the back door, the mare looked up at him; when he ignored her and rounded the house and started down the path, he heard her whinny. He smiled a little, stopped, and half-turning, called: "All right. Come on." There was an instant response, a short-lived clatter of hoofs, and the mare came whirling into view at the head of the path. When he turned his back on her and walked on, she came prancing down behind him, overtook him almost immediately, whinnied again, and poked him in the back with her nose. "All right, all right," he said to her and added, "You're a good girl. The best." She moved up alongside of him and trooped down to the corral with him and watched him climb up and perch himself on the top rail near the gate. He hunched forward with his boot heels hooked over the rail below him, his elbows resting on his knees and his hands clasped between them. She moved up to him again and nuzzled his hands. Suddenly her head jerked up and she stood motionlessly, a sign that he recognized. Her keen ears had heard something. Canavan raised his gaze. Coming across the open fields at a swift, pounding gallop was a horseman.

"Uh-huh," Canavan said half-aloud. "There he comes and judging by the way he's burning leather, he's madder'n a wet hen. Must've met Brady right after he left me and got the word from him. Wonder how much hollering he did."

As he sat back quietly and watched, Had Voight came steadily closer. Canavan lost sight of him for a couple of minutes when he was screened by the trees. But then he heard a horse snort, heard his hoofbeats louder than before, and presently Voight, a somewhat dark-faced man of forty or forty-five and average-sized, came riding down the path. He halted briefly when he came off it.

"Oh," Canavan heard him say when Voight spotted him. Voight jogged his horse down to the corral, and halted him as close to Canavan as he could get with the mare making no attempt to move and standing squarely between them. To add to Voight's annoyance—and his deepening frown indicated that he was annoyed—she turned herself, presenting her backside to him. Inwardly Canavan grinned a little. But then he gestured, and the mare, obeying him reluctantly, backed off a couple of steps, and Voight moved his horse up closer. Beyond lifting his eyes for an appraising look at him, Canavan sat quietly and waited for his uninvited caller to take the initiative.

The expression on Voight's face told him that this would not be a friendly encounter. Voight quickly confirmed it by asking grumpily: "You the new owner of this place?"

"That's right," Canavan replied, and thought to himself: "Oh-h, we're gonna hit it off just fine, this character and me."

"Didn't Stonebridge tell you that I had an agreement with Jake Spangler?"

"Nope."

"Well, he should have," Voight said heatedly.

"Maybe you oughta go see him about it," Canavan suggested.

"That would just be a waste of time. He'd tell me to see you. That's why I'm here."

Canavan made no response.

"Spangler agreed to let me water my stock at his stream and assured me our agreement would be honored by whoever bought the place after he disposed of it."

"Spangler give you that in writing?"

"He didn't have to!" Voight yelled. "He was a man of his word, and his word was good enough for me! What I want to know of you right here and now is what you intend to do about it."

"What I intend to do about it?" Canavan repeated.

"Yes!"

"I don't intend to do anything about it."

Voight glared at him, his eyes burning in his darkened face, and the muscles in his lean jaws twitching convulsively.

"For your information, mister," Canavan told him evenly, "assuming that there was such an agreement, even if Stonebridge had known about it and had told me about it, I wouldn't have gone for it. I'd never have made myself a party to anything so downright ridiculous. I've never heard of anyone giving somebody else, 'less maybe it was a son or a brother or some other kind of close relation, permission to run stock over his land and to use his water. But if you did have that kind of an arrangement with Spangler, what makes you think anybody else'd be fool enough to honor it? I won't, and that's for sure." He climbed down from his perch. "Y'wanna know something, Voight? Before you came storming over here, I'd just about decided that if you were nice an' friendly, maybe I'd stretch things a bit and let you go on watering here. Leastways till my own stock gets here. But you're anything but nice an' friendly. Fact is, you act so damned high and mighty, makes me wonder who the hell you think

21

you are? That's it, mister. You've said your piece and you've got your answer. Now suppose you haul yourself off my property and stay off? Go on now. Turn yourself around and start riding."

But Voight wasn't ready to go, not without firing a final shot. Stiffly erect in the saddle, his face a curious mixture of crimson-streaked black, he said: "My two grandfathers settled Indian Head. They wouldn't allow anyone here save their own. But in the last five or ten years we've taken a more tolerant attitude. We've accepted a handful of outsiders whom we considered desirable. But we've always rejected your kind, and we always will, as long as there's a Voight or a Thayer around to keep you out, and I'm sure there will be for a long, long time to come. You aren't wanted here. If you know what's good for you, you'll call off your deal with Stonebridge and clear out of Indian Head. If you don't—"

"Yeah?" Canavan chided him. "You'll what?"

"We'll run you out."

"You will, huh? Better men than you have tried that and they didn't get anywhere. But you think you're gonna do it. Don't make me laugh."

Voight backed his horse and wheeled him around.

"Hold it a minute," Canavan commanded, and Voight pulled up, and looked hard at him over his shoulder. "That kid, Paulie Voight . . ."

"What about him?"

"What's he to you? Your son?"

"Yes."

"I thought so. But not only because you two look so much alike. It's more than that. Something of you has rubbed off on him and that's too bad. Like you, he thinks who the hell he is. Kinda think he found out today that he isn't such a much. So you'd better think twice, Voight, before you go out of your way to hit back at me. If you don't, you'll find out what that smart alecky son of yours found out."

Voight didn't answer. Squaring around and settling himself in the saddle, he rode off. Minutes after he had gone, Canavan stepped up to the waiting mare and hoisted himself up on her. The mare trotted down the incline. When they reached the road, Canavan wheeled her and headed for town.

THREE

Stripped to the waist, his wet body glistening, Canavan stepped back from the washstand in his hotel room, caught up the towel that he had slung over the back of the room's only chair, and began to dry himself. There were slow, scuffing bootsteps outside on the landing; unconsciously he listened to them as he continued to towel himself. They came steadily closer. Then they stopped, and he did too and stood motionlessly, and waited. There was a moment-long pause, then a knock on the door. Drying his face and hands, Canavan crossed the room to the door and opened it. The landing was dimly lit, and the fact that his caller stood back from the door, out of range of the lamplight that reached only to the threshold, made immediate recognition impossible.

"Yeah?" Canavan asked. Suddenly he recognized the man. It was the sheriff. "Oh!" he said.

Peaseley grunted and said: "Got something to say to you, mister."

"All right," Canavan answered. "Say it," he added, plying the towel over his head and then draping it around his shoulders.

The sheriff coughed behind his hand, cleared his throat, pushed his spectacles a little higher up on his nose, and began with: "Kinda think, mister . . ."

"Name's Canavan."

"Huh? Oh, yeah . . . Canavan. Never was much of a hand remembering names. Easier remembering faces. Now where was I? Oh, yeah," he said a second time. "If I was a stranger in a strange town, and I was lookin' to settle there, the first thing I'd set out to do would be to make friends. But you don't go along with that idea, do you, mister?" This time even

23

though Peaseley's failure to call him by name made him frown, Canavan made no attempt to remind him of it. "Way I see it, you don't care a hoot if folks like you or if they don't. You've got yourself a reputation and you're gonna live up to it and the hell with anybody and everybody. I know you don't want 'ny advice outta me. All the same, though, I'm gonna give it to you. I'm the law around here. So that gives me the right to speak up whenever I've got something to say." When Canavan stood silently with his muscular, thick-wristed arms crossed over his chest and holding the ends of the towel together, the sheriff continued: "I didn't come up here to talk about the run-in you had with those three kids. I wasn't there, so I still don't know for sure what actu'lly did happen that made you gun th'm. All I know so far is what that blabber-mouth, Ossie Blue, said, and what you said. And while I don't think gunning those kids was the only way out of whatever it was that happened, long's you didn't kill any o' th'm, I won't make a to-do about it. Now what I came up here to see you about is a heckuva lot more important. It wouldn'ta hurt you none if you'da been a mite friendlier with Had Voight, and if you hadda told him he could go on watering his stock on the O-Bar same's he's been doing these past two years. Had's a big man 'round these parts, mister, and it don't pay to get him down on you."

"I'm hungrry, Peaseley, and you're keeping me from my supper," Canavan told him curtly. "So suppose you get outta here and let me get done so I can go get me something to eat?"

"All right. If that's the way you want it, that's the way it'll be," the sheriff said with a lift of his rounded shoulders. "But you're making a big mistake, mister, takin' that kind o' stand. Had Voight runs Indian Head, and everybody in it does as he says. You're a big man. But you aren't big enough to take him on and the whole town too." Peaseley paused and moistened his lips with the tip of his tongue. "I was hoping that being I'm so much older'n you, and chances are a mite wiser, and being that we have something in common, me being a lawman and you having been one, that you might listen t'me and take some friendly advice. But if you won't, you won't. Still, I'm sorry for you, mister."

"Thanks," Canavan retorted. "But don't waste your sympathy on me. Save it for somebody else, somebody who wants it and needs it."

Ignoring Canavan's retort, and apparently determined to have his full say, Peaseley added: "Wait till you need a friend around here and you find you haven't got one. And don't go thinking that Stonebridge is gonna buck Had and

24

the whole town for you. He won't because he knows which side his bread is buttered on. And wait till you wanna buy something here and you can't because nobody'll sell you, and when you set out to hire a crew to work your place and you don't find anybody willing to hire out to you. Oh-h, you've got a helluva lot to learn about dealing with people, mister. You'll learn. Only by then it'll probably be too late. If you've got a family somewhere and you've been planning to bring them out here, I wouldn't if I was you. Wouldn't be fair to th'm."

Canavan was a little late kicking the door shut, late because Peaseley had already turned and started for the stairs before Canavan lashed out at the door with his foot. Then as the departing lawman's plodding bootsteps faded out, Canavan, backed against the closed door with his broad shoulders spanning its width, thought angrily to himself: "That pussyfootin' old goat! Imagine me having something in common with the likes of him, the worst imitation of a lawm'n that I've ever met up with! As for Mister Had Voight, if he thinks he's gonna make me knuckle down to him by turning the town against me, he's got another think coming!"

He paced about briefly, grinding his big balled-up right fist into the palm of his left hand. Then he stopped, dropped the towel on the washstand, half of it in the partially filled bowl, the other half out, picked up the clean shirt that he had laid out for himself on the bed, donned it, and buttoned it up.

Some ten minutes later he strode into Ossie Blue's saloon, and again choosing the near end of the bar where it right-angled the back wall, headed for it. A man who was standing there toying with an empty foam-ringed beer glass looked up as Canavan neared the spot, then moved himself and his glass away. Ignoring the stares that other men in the place lifted to him, Canavan drummed on the wet surface of the bar with his fingers as he waited for Ossie.

While Ossie gave no sign that he had seen Canavan enter, when he was able to work his way up the bar, he placed a frothing glass of beer in front of Canavan, eyed him, and asked: "S'matter, partner? You look kinda sore. Somebody rub you the wrong way?"

"Got a minute?"

" 'Course."

"Tell me something about Had Voight."

Ossie's eyebrows arched a bit. "Oh-h, so that's it! Mean you an' him have tangled already?"

Canavan nodded. But he offered no further information.

"We-ll, let's see now. Had's pretty much the whole show here same's his father was and the old man's father before him. Trouble with Had is his temper and what he can't seem to forget, that he's a Voight. He's so, we-ll, impressed with being a Voight that he kinda looks down his nose at everybody else 'cept maybe the Thayers, and being that they're only cousins, I wouldn't wanna bet that he doesn't lay it into them same's he does to everybody else. Y'see, Canavan, nobody's ever had the guts to stand up to him. So that's kinda gone to his head, and now he expects everybody to kowtow to him. You come along and instead of knucklin' down to him, you probably did just the opposite and that musta set him back on his heels. So if I know Had the way I think I do, he'll have to do something about you. And that somebody he'll get after to take care of you will be his brother Alvah. Like everybody calls him Al for short, nobody calls Had by his right name, Hadley. But getting back to Al, he's got everything that Had wishes he had, a lot o' dough, a good-payin' spread, and the size to take care of anybody who gets in Had's way. That tell you enough?"

Canavan grinned a little. "More'n enough," he replied.

"Don't know if this c'n mean anything to you, but Paulie's Had's son. Only they're on the outs and have been for a long time. Y'see, Paulie's mother, Addie, and Had parted comp'ny some years ago, and Paulie, siding in with his mother, has lived with her ever since right up the street. Paulie hates Had's guts. They've tangled a couple o' times, Had and Paulie, but Had's never come off any better than a bad second best any o' those times. How bad was it, the run-in you had with Had?"

"He wanted me to agree to something that I couldn't see."

"That mean you only had words with him and that it didn't go past that?"

"Only words," Canavan answered. "Your friend the sheriff came around to see me just a while ago and—"

"My friend, huh?"

Canavan grinned again. "Maybe I shoulda said our friend. Anyway he seemed to think I should've let Had have what he wanted, and that because I didn't, I'm gonna find myself frozen out of just about everything in Indian Head. Nobody'll want any part o' me, the storekeepers won't sell me, and I won't be able to hire any hands. Even told me that if I have a family, it wouldn't be right of me or fair to th'm to bring them out here."

"That's nice," Ossie commented and looked troubled. "I don't norm'lly agree with anything that old goat says. Only this time I'm afraid he's right. Oh-h, I don't mean about you standing up to Had on whatever he wanted of you. I mean about people shyin' away from you, and about the storekeep-

26

ers refusing to do business with you. Most of them, y'know, are Voights, the others Thayers. And when Had cracks the whip, they jump. When he tells them not to sell you, they won't. They're that scared of him. So I'm afraid you're gonna find it rough going here, Canavan. And what you can do about it, I don't know."

"Oh, I'll make out somehow," Canavan assured him.

"I sure hope so."

"Had c'n run Indian Head. But that doesn't mean he runs any other place. What's the nearest town to this, how far is it from here, and which way is it?"

"That'd be Humboldt, the county seat," Ossie told him. "About thirty miles from here. When you ride out've here, head north for a couple o' miles, then begin to veer off kinda gradual like to the northwest. Keep going that way and you'll run right smack into it."

"Right," Canavan acknowledged. He gulped down his beer, dropped a coin on the bar, and added: "Thanks, Ossie. Thanks a lot."

The saloonkeeper smiled, a little wanly though, and said: "Any time, Canavan. Oh-h, case you're interested, I hear that the doc dug that slug of yours out of Paulie's shoulder, and that Paulie oughta be up and around again, say, in a couple o' weeks. No way of telling, though, if you beatin' him to the draw has made him any smarter, or if he aims to go after you soon's he feels up to it. 'Course he'll have lots o' time to think things over while he's laid up, and it could be he'll decide that being smart alecky, looking for trouble, and being top gun aren't worth it." When Canavan refrained from commenting, Ossie added: "As for that pesky Thayer kid, he'll never again have the full use of that wrist that you busted for 'im. The bullet you pegged at him shattered the wrist bone. So from now on he's gonna have to practice and learn to do things for himself lefty." Quite suddenly his face clouded. "Oh-oh."

"S'matter?" Canavan asked him.

"Al Voight and two of his hands. They're standing outside. Al looked in. Now he's sayin' something to the other two. They're coming in."

Canavan nodded and said: "Think you'd better move down the bar, Ossie. I don't want you getting yourself mixed up in this."

Ossie needed no urging. Turning away from Canavan, he started down the bar, stopped long enough to reach out and take a couple of empty glasses that were held out to him, and went on. He dipped the glasses into a bucket of water beneath the level of the bar, dipped them a second time, finally flushing out the foam that ringed their insides, refilled them with beer and returned them to the men who held out their hands for them.

Hunched over the bar and toying with his empty glass, rolling it gently between his big hands, Canavan was aware of movement past him to the bar. Stealing a quick look, he saw three men, one a big, beefy man whom he knew had to be Al Voight, and two others of far less imposing size, come up to the bar and lean over it. As they did, Canavan lowered his eyes.

"Beer, Ossie. Three o' th'm."

"Coming right up, Al," Ossie responded.

Still toying with his glass, Canavan could feel eyes fixed upon him.

"You, Mac," the man who had ordered the beer said.

Taking it for granted that he was the one whom Al had addressed, but pretending to be unaware of it, Canavan ignored him. Then, even though his gaze was averted, Canavan glimpsed Ossie serving the big man and his companions.

"Hey, you," Al said again, and added, "I mean you, Red."

Canavan gave no sign that he had heard him.

"Must be deaf or something, Al," one of Voight's companions said shortly.

"Tell him I'm talkin' to him, Ossie," Al ordered.

"Yeah, sure."

Still playing his little game of pretense, and abandoning it only when he had no alternative, it was only when the saloonkeeper touched his arm that Canavan raised his head.

"Yeah?" he asked.

"Man over there is talkin' to you," Ossie told him, and he nodded at Al.

"Oh?" Canavan said, and turning his head, leveled a look at the bulky Voight.

The latter frowned. "You deaf or something?" he demanded.

"Nope. Are you?"

Al's frown deepened into a scowl. "Don't get smart with me," he retorted gruffly. "I know who you are. Case you don't know who I am, I'll tell you. I'm Al Voight. I'm fixin' to water some o' my brother Had's stock on the O-Bar t'morrow morning."

"Just like that, huh?"

"That's right. Just like that. What are you gonna do about it?"

"Why don't you wait till then and see?"

"I don't wanna wait. I asked you a question and I want an answer now."

28

"I gave you an answer. But if you didn't hear it, if you don't hear so good, I'll repeat it. Wait'll tomorrow and see."

The big man glared at him for a moment.

"All right, mister," he said finally. "You be there when I come by tomorrow morning."

"Oh, I'll be there, all right," Canavan answered. "You can count on it. Wanna warn you, though, that you'll be trespassing, and you know as well as I do that when a man trespasses on another man's property, he's liable to get himself shot. But if you're in such a sweat to join your ancestors ahead o' time, it'll be all right with me. The minute I spot you on my land, I'll put a nice big lead slug right smack in that potbelly of yours, and before you die you'll be able to see what your guts look like when they spill out of you."

"You . . . you want another beer?" Ossie asked him.

"No," Canavan said, and pushed the glass in front of him into Ossie's hands.

"Drink up, boys," Al Voight said to his companions, "and let's get out of here."

The three drained their glasses and put them down again, and each wiped his mouth with the back of his hand. Al produced a handful of coins, dropped a couple of them on the bar, gave Canavan a hard look, and led the way out.

The moment the three men had left the place, there was a loud whispering among the standees at the bar. Canavan, straightening up, caught Ossie's eye as he stepped back from the bar, and gave him a half-salute as he turned to go. He stopped when Ossie motioned to him to wait, retraced his steps to the bar, and waited till the saloonkeeper came hurrying up along the bar and leaned over it.

"You don't scare easy," Ossie said. "All the same, don't make the mistake of thinking that Al does, because he doesn't. I know he sounds off a lot and big sometimes. But we've had our share of badmen come through here over the years and I've seen Al take them on two and sometimes three at a time and beat hell out of them. So I know he isn't afraid of doing what he sets out to do. Kinda late, don't you think, for you to head out tonight for Humboldt? One thing if you knew the country. But being that you don't . . ."

"I've been thinking the same thing, Ossie. And being that I wanna be on hand when Al shows up tomorrow morning, guess I'd better not take any chances of finding myself lost in the middle of nowhere and wind up having to stay put there till dawn so's I can figure out which way I oughta go. So I'll put it off till sometime tomorrow. Now if I could only find some place where I could get me something to eat . . ."

"You'll find my supper settin' on the table in the back

room," Ossie told him, pointing to the rear. "Had it brought in just before you came in. I'm not hungry. And if I am later on I've got stuff in there that I c'n fix. So g'wan. Eat it before it gets 'ny colder and it has to be thrown out."

Heads turned in his direction as he made his way to the rear and into the tiny cubicle that served as an office for Ossie. And when he emerged half an hour later, heads turned again, but as before he simply stared back stonily. Ossie looked up, caught his eye, and when Canavan nodded and patted his stomach, the saloonkeeper smiled.

Halting in the open doorway for a moment and lifting his gaze skyward, Canavan debated with himself whether to get his gear and the mare and ride out to the O-Bar and spend the night there, or turn in, since he had nothing better to do, and enjoy a good night's sleep in his hotel bed—or as good a sleep as the lumpy, thin-worn mattress would allow. He would arise early and ride out to the O-Bar and be on hand for Al Voight's expected and promised appearance. If he chose to ride out to the O-Bar that night, he would have to sleep in the open with his blanket serving two purposes, mattress and covering for him, while his saddle would have to become a pillow. It wouldn't be the first time that he had had to do that, and it probably wouldn't be the last.

He was still debating with himself when there was a sudden spiteful crack of a rifle. Instinctively he hunched down, just as a bullet plowed into the wooden framework above the doorway and spewed a handful of gouged-out splinters over him. Instinctively too his right hand dropped and when it jerked upward again, his gun was in his hand. He suddenly realized that by standing in the open doorway with brightly burning lamplight from the saloon silhouetting him, he was targeting himself for another shot from his hidden assailant. Crouching low with his gun raised for a quick shot, he glided out of the doorway and skidded to an awkward stop in the entrance to a dark alley alongside the saloon. Flattening out against the wall, he inched forward cautiously and peered out, ranging a quick look across the street for a sign of the rifleman. The houses and the stores opposite the saloon were thoroughly darkened. But then his keen, probing eyes spied a shadowy figure, a man's, rise up from the rooftop of one of the stores. Instantly Canavan's gun leveled and roared. The man seemed to straighten up for a moment as Canavan watched him, suddenly swayed, and just as suddenly lurched forward and toppled off the roof and crashed heavily on the walk below. Something fell with him and landed on the walk close by him. Canavan was quite certain that it was a rifle.

There was a rush of booted feet. Men burst out of the

saloon; those in the lead stopped so suddenly on the walk that those behind them piled into them and trampled them as they sought the source of the gunfire. When they spotted the sprawled-out figure across the street, they dashed over. Now other men attracted by the shooting came running from different directions. Converging upon the spot where Canavan's hapless victim lay, they helped swell the crowd that had begun to gather around.

As Canavan holstered his gun and came erect and sauntered out of the alley, Ossie Blue, probing his shattered doorway with his fingers, spied him and called to him. "Hey, Canavan! Somebody take a shot at you?"

"That's right," Canavan replied, turning and joining Ossie in the doorway. "I ducked into the alley and waited and when the polecat showed himself—"

"You got him."

"Didn't want him to take another shot at me."

A couple of men, obviously some of those who had been drinking in Ossie's place, broke out of the still-swelling crowd and came trudging back. As the first man stepped up on the walk, Ossie asked him: "Who's that layin' over there?"

"That snotty Simmons kid," was the reply. "That's what happens when young squirts like him take to wearin' guns and think that makes th'm men." Then addressing himself to Canavan, he asked: "You the one he took a shot at?"

"Uh-huh."

"He won't do it again. He's dead."

FOUR

While Ossie Blue and his returning customers trooped back into the saloon, Canavan lingered outside, idling on the walk in front of it, his eyes holding on the crowd that was milling about across the street. When three men carrying what appeared to be a wooden door came trudging out of a nearby alley, the crowd gave way before them; when the dead body of youthful Curly Simmons was lifted onto the door, a fourth man joined the other three and helped them carry it away. Then the crowd began to break up.

A man who was among the last to leave and who walked with a wearied, labored step and who was clutching a rifle in his right hand, plodded across the street, mounted the walk, and halted squarely in front of Canavan. The man was the sheriff. He pushed his spectacles higher up on his nose, rubbed his nose with the back of his hand, and cleared his throat.

"We-ll, here we go again," Canavan thought to himself. Then, suddenly deciding to put Peaseley on the defensive, he said gravely: "I've been wondering about you, Peaseley. You put that kid up to potshottin' me?"

The sheriff stared at him, his mouth opening and his jaw hanging. He closed his mouth and gulped and swallowed hard.

"Why, doggone you," he sputtered. "You ... you've sure got a helluva gall accusing me of—"

"So maybe it wasn't your idea," Canavan continued, ignoring Peaseley's protestation. "I'm not so sure that you ever had an idea of your own. Maybe it was your boss, Had Voight, who came up with the idea and told you to talk that fool kid into trying it. On the other hand, because there has to be a first time for everything, maybe it was your idea. I

32

know you don't like me and that you'd like to get rid o' me because every time you look at me you realize what a lousy imitation of a lawman you are. So . . ."

Peaseley glared at him. "Wanna tell you something, mister," he retorted. "And I don't give a damn if you believe it or if you don't. I didn't have anything to do with what that boy did. I'm willing to own up to not liking you or what you stand for. But that's all. Oh, 'cept for one thing, and that is the sooner you clear out've Indian Head, the better everybody, and that includes me, will like it."

"You'd better get used to having me around, Peaseley. Because I'm staying put."

The sheriff eyed him in silence for a moment, then he began with: "We've had more excitement in your one day here than any I c'n remember. And that's going back a long, long ways. You started off by gunnin' down those two boys, then you acted up with Had Voight, followed that by telling Al Voight that you'll kill him if he goes through with what he said he's gonna do tomorrow morning. Then you kill a kid when you could've winged him instead. All in all, I'd say you've had a mighty busy time of it, wouldn't you?"

"I didn't know it was a kid up on that roof. All I could see was a shadowy figure. Kids don't usu'lly go 'round taking potshots at people, so I didn't have any reason to think it was a kid. So being that I don't like being shot at, when he raised up, I fired at him."

"And killed him with your one shot. If you're that good a shot in the dark, how come you didn't wing him instead of killing him?"

"You keep harpin' on that and I keep tellin' you I didn't know it was a kid, and where'll that get us?"

"I still don't see why you had to kill him," the sheriff persisted.

Canavan looked hard at him. "Why don't you go on about your business, Peaseley, and leave me alone?"

"From now on you call me Sheriff Peaseley."

"I'm kinda sorry it wasn't you up on that roof instead of that Simmons kid."

"Yeah, I'll bet you are. Mister, I'm gonna give you a tip. I'm gonna ride herd on you. I'm gonna watch you like a hawk. You do anything that doesn't look just right to me, I'll take you in so fast, it'll make your head swim. Now you put that in your pipe and smoke it."

"I've got a tip for you, Peaseley."

"Yeah?" was the taunting response.

"You keep getting in my hair, and I'll take that tin star of yours and shove it down your throat."

33

"Long's we know where we stand with each other, that kinda, we-ll, simplifies things," the sheriff answered with surprising calm. "Only the way I see it, it's gonna be a helluva lot easier for me to do what I said I'd do than it will be for you. Whether you like it or not, I'm the law around here. So whatever I do will be in the . . . the line of duty. Of keepin' the peace. And if that means killing you for resisting arrest, I'll do that. Now you think that one over, mister."

"Get out of my way," Canavan said, and pushed him off and sauntered away up the street.

He had had enough of Indian Head. He wouldn't spend the night there after all. He would ride out to the O-Bar where he belonged, and he would make it his business to avoid coming into town.

"Long's Had Voight and that pussyfootin' sheriff of his run this lousy town, I'll stay the hell away from it," he thought bitterly to himself. "I don't want any part of it. And when I have to get anything, I'll ride over to Humboldt and get it. Right now I'm gonna get my horse, pick up my gear from the hotel, and clear out."

He lengthened his stride as he marched on. The long street, he noticed, was quiet, and save for the glary, yellowish lamplight that streamed out of the saloons, it was steeped in deepening darkness. The sound of liquor-thickened voices and snatches of raucous laughter drifted out of the saloons. But the loud voices and the laughter were short-lived, and the silence returned.

Canavan's bootheels thumped rhythmically on the planked walk, the only sound to beat against the silence. Unconsciously he glanced across the street as he neared the bank. Movement in the entrance to the gloomily dark alleys that flanked it attracted his attention, and he slowed his step instinctively, wondering the while if he had actually spotted moving figures in the alleys, or if he had imagined it. When he saw a shadowy figure peer out of one alley and caught a bare, fleeting glimpse of another man do the same thing from the other alley, he knew he hadn't imagined anything. Then he saw a flickering light burn briefly inside the bank itself.

Deliberately then, so as to avoid arousing the suspicions of the two men who he was sure were watching him, he walked on. Then as he neared a dark alley diagonally opposite the bank, he slanted across the walk and turned into the alley and promptly collided, heavily too, with someone. Instinctively they pushed each other off.

"What are you tryin' to do?" the shadowy man whom Canavan had trampled demanded. "Climb all over me?"

"Sorry," Canavan retorted sarcastically. "Only next time

34

when you hear someone coming, and chances are you saw me too, get out of the way."

"Hold it now," the man commanded. "For a minute there I wasn't sure. Now I think I am. I think I know who you are."

"And I think I know who you are. All you Voights sound alike."

"'You're Canavan, aren't you?"

"Yeah. And you're the little king's big brother. What'd you do, hustle over to that pussyfootin' imitation of a sheriff and complain to him about me warning you to stay off my place and what I said I'd do to you if you—?"

"I didn't complain about you or anybody else to Ab Peaseley," Al Voight said heatedly, interrupting Canavan. "He wanted to know what we'd said to each other and I told him. Know what's going on across the street?"

"Looks to me like the bank's being robbed."

"Right. There are five o' th'm in on the job. Two are inside, two are standing guard in the alleys, and the fifth one's minding the horses up the street near the corner. Understand you were a lawman once, Texas Ranger, wasn't it? Then you musta run into all kinds of law breakin' including bank robbing. Wanna give me a hand here? Between us we might be able to break it up. What d'you say?"

"I owe Stonebridge something for talking up for me. So all right. I'll give you a hand. But if it was for anybody else, one o' you high an' mighty Voights or one of the Thayers, I wouldn't lift a finger to stop it."

"We aren't as bad as you think we are, Canavan. And I'm willing to admit that Had shouldn'ta talked to you the way he did. But that's his way, and there isn't anything that anybody c'n do about it."

"You haven't said so, Voight, leastways not right out. But I kinda think you know he was way outta line the way he came at me with that cock-'n-bull story about Spangler telling him that he'd see to it that whoever bought the O-Bar would let him go on watering his stock there. And for that matter, you're just as bad as he is, telling me you're gonna take over for him and drive his herd over my land, and then wanting to know what I aimed to do about it. Way I see it, you Voights have been lordin' it over people for so long, and gettin' away with it, that you've come to expect everybody to knuckle down to you. I won't, and you c'n bet your last buck on it too. What's more, I'll give you two as good as you give me and maybe more. C'mon, we've got business to attend to. So let's get at it."

Both drew their guns and stepped away from each other, Voight to one side of the alley, Canavan to the other.

Crouching down and shoulder-nudging the building wall on their respective sides, with their eyes fixed on the bank and their guns half-raised and ready, they waited. Voight stole a look in Canavan's direction. But the deep, gloomy darkness was impenetrable. He couldn't see Canavan.

"So damned dark in here," he said. "Can't even see you. You all set?"

"Yeah, sure," Canavan replied. "All set."

"You gonna say when to shoot?"

"Uh-huh."

"Who d'we take first? The two on the outside, or the two who are cleanin' out the place?"

"We'll wait till the two inside come out, and then when they're all together, we'll pour it into th'm."

"Right!"

The bank door opened and Canavan promptly hissed at Al Voight: "Here they come!"

They saw a man poke his head out and steal a quick look upstreet and then down. Apparently satisfied that no one was aware of what was going on in the bank, he turned his head, obviously to say something to someone behind him, and with his hand on his gun, stepped out on the walk. The someone behind him, a man who was carrying what looked to be a heavy box, appeared in the doorway, and turned sideways in order to maneuver himself and the box out at the same time. As he stepped outside, the two men who had been posted in the flanking alleys emerged and joined the first man, who was standing at the curb and looking upstreet. After a moment he whistled and beckoned vigorously. The man with the box joined his companions and all four turned their gaze upstreet as hoofbeats sounded.

Voight, raising up a bit, looked at Canavan.

"Now!" the latter said at that very moment.

Firing together, the two blasted the waiting bank robbers. The man who had whistled and who appeared to be the leader of the band tumbled into the gutter while the man with the box staggered and dropped it and sprawled over it. The other two men, spotting the source of the gun flashes, fired back. But the fire from the alley was far deadlier since Canavan and Voight, hidden from view of the robbers by the obscuring darkness, had targets at which to shoot. One of the two surviving bandits, firing from a half bent-over position, was hit squarely, and stumbled backward. Careening across the walk, he stopped when he collided with one of the bank's windows, lay back against it for a moment or two, then straightening up, raised his gun for another shot. Hit solidly again, fatally this time, he dropped his gun and stumbled away blindly, and fell sideways into the open doorway and across the threshold. The fourth man, holstering his gun, bent over the strongbox and came erect with it in his arms just as a mounted man leading four riderless horses behind him came dashing up. The two men, the one standing on the curb and the horseman, managed to hoist the heavy box onto the back of one of the horses. While the mounted man held the box in place, the other man hauled himself up into the saddle. Abandoning the unneeded horses, the two, lashing their own horses with the loose ends of the reins, sent them bounding away. A withering blast of gunfire that emptied Canavan's and Voight's guns overtook the fleeing robbers and spilled both of them into the gutter. Their horses ran on a bit farther, stopped and looked back, turned and trotted back, halted when they came to where their riders lay, and standing over them, whinnied. One of the horses plodded over to sniff and nudge the strongbox that had crashed so heavily. He backed away from it shortly and retraced his steps to stand again over his fallen rider.

Reloading their guns as they emerged from the entrance to the alley, the point from which they had fired their last two shots, Canavan and Voight halted briefly on the walk. Lights began to flicker and finally burn steadily in windows all along the street, on both sides of it too, and here and there the more curious of the awakened citizenry raised their windows and poked their heads out. One man with rumpled hair leaned far out of an upper floor window. Spotting Canavan and Voight standing together diagonally opposite him, he hollered: "Hey, you fellers! What's goin' on?"

"Huh?" Voight asked with feigned innocence. "What d'you mean?"

"All that gunplay!" the man yelled. "S'matter, you deaf or something that you didn't hear it?"

"What say?" Voight asked, cupping his left hand around his left ear.

"Ah-h, the hell with it!" the man hollered.

He withdrew his head and slammed down his window. A moment later the light behind him went out.

"Sounded kinda mad, didn't he?" Voight asked.

"Yeah, I think he was, being that he didn't bother to say good night."

They could see men coming from different directions. Those who were fully dressed came from the saloons; the others, those who had pulled on their pants and boots but who hadn't taken the time to put on their shirts, were the rudely awakened ones. While their wives were content to see what they could from their windows, their more curious menfolk

37

refused to be satisfied with that and hurried out to get a firsthand view of things. Some gathered around the two dead men who lay in the gutter; others, after a more or less mechanical glance at them, headed for the bank where the biggest crowd had already begun to assemble and where there was greater excitement.

"Don't see 'ny sign of that flannel-mouthed old goat of a sheriff," Canavan observed. "Bet when he heard the first shot fired, he got under his bed and stayed put there. And now that it's over, he'll pop up and make out like he had a hand in breaking the thing up. How'd he get the job anyway? Don't tell me he was elected to it. It was Had's doing, wasn't it, Had who picked him and who pinned the star on him?"

"I wouldn't know. I never asked and nobody ever told me. But Ab isn't the worst kind around. Oh, I know he's old and kinda crotchety . . ."

"And he listens to Had like he was God and follows his orders like he got th'm from up above. We-ll, I'm getting out of here. The O-Bar's where I belong and that's where I'll stay," Canavan said, settling his hat more securely on his head. Curling the brim with his big hands, he shot a look at Voight, who stood a little spread-legged with his thumbs hooked in his belt and who was watching the aimless milling about across the street. "Am I gonna see you tomorrow morning?"

"I said I'd be there, didn't I?"

"That's what you said."

"Then you c'n count on me being there."

"Then you're an even bigger fool than I thought," Canavan answered angrily.

Voight turned his head and grinned at him. "What makes you so sure you're gonna kill me and that I won't kill you instead?"

Ignoring his question, Canavan said: "Before you head out for my place, you'd better make your arrangements with whoever it is around here who does the fixin' up and the burying to come and get you. I don't want you layin' around my place and rotting and stinkin' it up for me."

"Y'know, Canavan, if I kill you, that'll be the end of it. Nobody'll make anything out of it, and sooner than you think, you and it'll be forgotten. But if you kill me, Had'll never let up on you till he sees you swing for killing me. That's what happens when you're a stranger in a strange place and you try to buck those who were there ahead of you. You can't win. One way or another they wind up getting you. It isn't a matter of right or wrong. It's just the way things have to be."

Topping the incline and with the barn just ahead of them, Canavan brought the unprepared mare to an abrupt stop when he spotted a flickering light gleaming for a moment in one of the upper floor windows. He frowned and muttered: "Looks like I've got some uninvited company."

He dismounted and led the mare up to the barn. He backed her into the deep, concealing shadows that the towering structure cast off, dropped the reins at her feet, loosened the gun in his holster, and strode off. Circling the ramp that upgraded to the barn door, he followed the wall of the building to its very end. Then he took to the cushioning grass that carpeted the ground under the arching trees, and went on till he was past the veranda. He emerged from the trees and glided across the path to the house. Reaching it, and hugging the side of the house, he followed the path, bending low whenever he came to a window. As he rounded the house to the rear, something that loomed up quite suddenly squarely ahead of him stopped him in his tracks. Drawn up close to the back door, in fact within a short stride of it, was a buckboard with a team of horses idling in its traces. His expression reflected his surprise.

"Can't be what I thought it might," he told himself, "a bunch of Voights an' Thayers layin' for me and ready to jump me. They wouldn't have come in a buckboard." Then, rubbing the bristly point of his chin with the back of his hand: "Now who in blazes—?"

His conjecturing was short-lived. The back door opened and he beat a hasty retreat, backing around the house to the head of the path. With his drawn gun in his hand, he peered out and waited for his visitors to come out.

The door creaked a little as it was opened wide. A cloaked woman with the hood raised over her head and held together tightly to conceal her face stepped outside and ranged a quick, guarded look about her. After a moment she turned her head and said something over her shoulder that Canavan couldn't make out to someone whom he couldn't see. She stepped up to the buckboard, half-turned, and waited. A man came out of the house, quietly closed the door behind him, shifted something that he was carrying in his right arm to the hollow of his left, and stepped up next to the waiting woman. It was a folded-up blanket that he was carrying, Canavan decided. The man put it under the wide seat of the buckboard, helped the woman climb up and settle herself with her full skirts tucked in behind her legs, then he climbed up too and seated himself at her side. He unwound the lines from around the handbrake, released the handbrake, but instead of wheeling around the house and down the path and the incline to the road that led to town, he drove off, heading away over the open fields.

"How d'you like that for gall?" Canavan muttered indignantly. "Using my house for a hotel. Bet they're Voights. Nobody else would have that much gall. For their sake, I hope they don't make this a habit. If they try it again, they won't like what I tell th'm."

FIVE

Canavan awoke with a start. Someone was doing something to him and was not being too gentle about it. When he dared open his eyes, he found himself face-to-face with the mare, who was bending over him and nuzzling him.

"Why, you sonuvagun," he said.

He reached up and patted her affectionately and she whinnied softly. But when she sought to nuzzle him again, he pushed her away, kicked off the confining blanket, and struggled up into a sitting position. He yawned and stretched himself.

It was dawn, a damp and chilly dawn too. Everything about him was dew-wet. He hauled himself up, and as the backed-off mare watched him, he stamped about in an effort to get the blood circulating again. He swung his arms and rubbed them vigorously, rubbed his thighs and the calves of his legs too, twisted from side to side, even hunched up his shoulders and punched away at an imaginary opponent as he worked the stiffness out of his body.

When he bent over to roll up his blanket it felt damp to the touch. He bunched it up in his arms and carried it over to the corral, flipped it open, and draped it over the top rail to dry out under the sun's rays. He saddled the mare, hoisted himself up on her back, and wheeled her away. Minutes later he was drumming over the empty fields with the sweet smell of the thick, lush grass lifting and filling the air with its richness. Widely spaced clusters of wild flowers added their own fragrance.

When he came to the fence that marked the property line between Had Voight's place and the O-Bar, he slowed the mare to a trot and rode along it, looking for breakthroughs.

There were several that he spotted. But because they were of a minor nature, he simply glanced at them and rode on. But then he came upon a great gap in the fence, and promptly pulled up.

"Uh-huh," he said half-aloud, slacking a bit in the saddle. "This must be where Had's stock has been coming through."

The fence posts had been uprooted and tossed aside; heaped-up coils of rusted wire lay about practically everywhere. The grass in the area of the breakthrough was trampled, and on every side of him there were easily readable and recognizable tracks, some of them horses', but in the main they were the split hoof prints of lumbering cattle.

He backed the mare off a bit, climbed down, and dropped the reins at her feet. Fortunately, he quickly discovered, the post holes had not been filled in. As the mare watched, he set about "replanting" the posts. Using a good-sized rock with which to do the job, he hammered the posts, one after another, down into the holes from which they had been torn out. Then he caught up the nearest coil of wire and proceeded to restring the upper strand, crossing over onto Voight's property each time he needed more wire. It was slow, hard-on-the-hands-and-back work that was made even more difficult than it should have been because of the refusal of the rusted wire to cooperate with him in his efforts to disentangle it. It yielded to him eventually, though begrudgingly. He was wheezing and chest-heaving when he finished restringing the bottom strand.

Backing off to the mare's side, and ranging a critical eye over the restrung fence, aware that it was pretty much of a makeshift job, he turned shortly and climbed up on her. He yanked his rifle out of the saddleboot, and holding it across his knees, sat back and waited. From time to time the mare, apparently anxious to be off and doing, turned her head and looked around at him as though she was wondering what they were waiting for. When Canavan ignored her, she snorted and pawed the ground with her hoof; when these antics failed to produce the desired result, she tossed her head. When Canavan suddenly jerked back on the reins and spoke sharply to her, she subsided. She grumbled some, though, deep down in her throat; when he spoke to her a second time, she stood quietly, his tone of voice cautioning her not to continue her antics. For a while she stood, head bowed. Then she raised her head, just as an approaching horseman, heading straight for the fence, came into view. When she whinnied softly, Canavan patted her, and said: "It's all right. I see him."

The mounted man came steadily closer. But he was still too far off to be recognized. Taking it for granted that it was Al

42

Voight, Canavan thought grimly to himself: "We-ll, here comes the showdown. And I was hoping that there wouldn't have to be one with him. Kinda thought that he and I could get along. Same's I was hoping that after he'd slept on it the damned fool might get some sense into that thick skull of his and change his mind about crowding me into a gun fight with him. Guess the sooner I realize that all Voights are alike, downright pigheaded and stupid, the better off I'll be."

He held his narrowed, bitter-eyed gaze on the oncoming horseman, held it on him as he came loping up to within a hundred yards or so of the patched-up fence, and looked thoroughly surprised when he saw that it was the sheriff and not Al Voight.

"Wonder what old flannel-mouth is doing here?" he asked himself.

He continued to sit quietly astride the mare, and gave no sign of recognition when Peaseley came loping up to the fence and brought his panting horse to a stop. Ranging his eyes over the restrung wire, Peaseley finally lifted his gaze to Canavan and called out to him: "See you a minute?"

Canavan made no immediate reply. Then after a moment he asked rather gruffly: "What about?"

"Y'mind coming over here? Won't cost you anything to hear what I've gotta say."

Deliberately holding the mare in check, Canavan walked her across the twenty feet of intervening space to the fence. Thumbing his battered hat up from his forehead and clearing his throat behind his upraised dirty fingernailed hand, the sheriff said: "Now before you go getting ideas, say, like you scared Al Voight outta keeping his word, I think I'd better tell you right off that you didn't. Fact is, he was all set to show up here with Had's herd. I talked him into stayin' put till after I'd had a word with you. Indian Head has always been willing to bend over backwards to keep things quiet and peaceable, and I'm hoping I c'n get you to go along with us on that."

"Get to the point, Peaseley," Canavan said curtly, "and never mind anything else. But if you came over here thinking you could sweet-talk me into anything, save your breath and your time and go back to Had's and tell Al I'm waiting for him."

The sheriff bristled a bit, but controlled himself and sputtered: "I didn't come over here to sweet-talk you. Came over to tell you that Indian Head's obliged to you for helping Al put a stop to robbing the bank. That goes for all of us same's it does for Stonebridge. Being that what you did was so, well, decent, in fact, neighborly y'might even call it, why in thunder

43

can't we go on from there friendly-like and work out something between Had and you, huh?"

"Indian Head doesn't owe me anything and I don't owe Indian Head anything. So what I did wasn't for Indian Head. Only for Stonebridge because I felt I owed him a little something, and saving his bank and his money was my way of squaring things with him. If it had been somebody else who owned the bank, I wouldn't have raised a finger to stop those five mavericks. They could've cleaned out the place and they could've taken it apart piece-by-piece and carted it away, for all it would've mattered to me. Now getting back to what brought you over here, how many times do I have to tell you that nobody's gonna run cattle over my property?"

Peaseley's rounded shoulders lifted a bit.

"All right, mister. If you think you c'n buck a lot o' folks and live to tell about it you're gonna find out that it can't be done. No one man, no matter how big and tough he is and how good he is with his gun, c'n take on a whole county and beat it. Now don't get me wrong. I'm the law and the law doesn't take sides even though I'm with Indian Head all the way. What I'm trying to do is point out to you how wrong you are, and I'm doing it for your good, not mine, because whatever you do and whatever happens to you won't be any skin offa my nose. Only offa yours."

Backing his horse away from the fence, the sheriff wheeled around and rode off in the same direction from which he had come. Canavan followed him with bitter eyes. Then, as Peaseley and his horse faded away in the brightening distance, Canavan backed the mare as he had earlier and resumed his vigil.

"Damned old goat," he muttered darkly. "Never knew anybody who got under my hide the way he does. If I could just wallop him once, I'd feel better. But he's too old. So I can't do that. Oh, why in blazes did Elena have to know Stonebridge? Why couldn't it have been somebody else instead of him and some other place instead of this one?"

The mare's head jerked around suddenly and she whinnied, and Canavan, still frowning, twisted around and looked back too. Coming toward him at a swift lope, the thick grass muffling the rhythmic beat of his horse's hoofs, was a mounted man who rode loosely and effortlessly in the saddle. Canavan leveled a wondering look at him. As the man came steadily closer, Canavan turned the mare and sat back and waited for the stranger to come up to him. He did shortly, a long, lean individual with twinkling blue eyes set in a lined, sun-bronzed face, and a touch of gray showing in his sideburns.

Pulling up squarely in front of Canavan, he said: "Elena

thought you'd be somewhere around the place and sent me out to find you. She said if I spotted a big man with red hair and who looked as Irish as his name, that he'd be the one I was looking for. You're big all right, and I can see the red hair, and if a Bannon can't spot another Irishman when he sees one, then—"

"Y'mean Elena's here?" Canavan asked eagerly.

"Just got here. As I was ridin' off to look for you, I saw her and that Mexican woman of hers, that Maria, heading for the house to have a look around inside."

Shoving his rifle down in the saddleboot, Canavan cast a quick look over his shoulder and wondered why Al Voight hadn't appeared yet, and hoped that since he hadn't he wouldn't till he, Canavan, returned. Squaring around in the saddle, he said to Bannon: "Let's go."

Bannon wheeled around after Canavan and ranged his horse alongside the mare. For a minute or so the two men rode on in silence. Then Bannon, turning to Canavan, said: "In case you're wondering how I come to know Elena, and I'm sure you must be, I was ramrod for the Mitchells, neighbors of Elena's folks, back in Oklahoma. She was only a sprout when I first saw her, a cute one though, even though she was all freckles and as leggy as a colt. But even then the signs were there that she'd be something to knock your eye out when she grew up, and from what I saw four days ago when I ran into her in Truxton, I'd read the signs right. You've got y'self quite a pretty little lady there, Canavan. Think you'll have to look far an' wide to find another one like her."

"I know that, Bannon," Canavan answered. "Elena took you on?"

"She said if I was willing to come along with her and take my chances on having you say you c'n use me . . ."

"If Elena says you're all right, that's good enough for me."

"Thanks. I know I'll like working for her, and since I know about you from Elena, I kinda think that running into her was my lucky day. Oh-h, there are four o' my boys with Elena. When the Mitchells sold out, we kinda figured we'd head for California. But if you c'n use them too . . ."

"I sure can. Fact is, the five of you have been on the payroll since you started out with Elena. I'm tickled to death to know that Elena didn't have to make it out here alone and that you and your boys were along to see that nothing happened to her."

That was the extent of their conversation. Bannon looked quite pleased while Canavan wore an expression of unconcealed relief. To have a crew to work the O-Bar handed to

45

him on a silver platter, when he had already begun to wonder if he would ever be able to hire any hands in view of what Had Voight and his echo, Ab Peaseley, had predicted, meant that he had scored his first triumph over them. With a competent crew on hand he could now turn his attention to stocking the O-Bar with cattle.

"Oh-h, they won't like it," he thought to himself, his eyes gleaming, "when they find out about it. But I'm gonna like it all the more because of them and how they're gonna feel about it."

Too occupied with his thoughts, he did not realize that he had eased up on the reins. The fleet-footed mare, proud of her ability to outrun any horse that had ever been pitted against her and anxious to show Bannon's horse that he didn't class with her, quickly took advantage of Canavan's unconscious lapse and promptly bounded ahead. Bannon's bay, refusing to concede anything to her, pounded away after her. For a while it was fairly even with the bay managing to hold his own with her. But when he began to labor and falter, Bannon quickly checked him, and Canavan, suddenly becoming aware of what was going on, pulled back on the reins, slowing the mare to a more normal pace. Put out with him for interfering just when she was about to leave the panting, heaving, heavy-hoofed bay far behind her, she snorted furiously and fought for her head. But Canavan refused to give in to her. He maintained his strong grip on the taut reins, and forced her to resume the steady lope with which they had begun the return to the house. Once again the still-wheezing bay pulled alongside of her. She shrilled and trumpeted nasally and flashed him a scornful look. He ignored it and loped along with her.

When they rode around the screening trees and broke into the open at the rear of the house, Canavan slid down even before the mare had come to a full stop. He ran to the back door, skidded to an instant stop, caught Elena in his arms as she was coming out, lifted her, and kissed her hard on the mouth.

With her arms curled around his neck, she drew back her head, laughed lightly, and said: "Hello."

"Hello yourself," he answered, and kissed her hard again.

When she was again able to draw back her head, she said gravely, although her happy, shining eyes belied her tone: "Apparently you don't know it, but there are people who frown upon such exhibitions of affection between old married people like us."

"That so?" he asked, and kissed the tip of her nose.

"Oh, yes," she said as gravely as before.

"G'wan," he said, still holding her tight in his arms. "Don't put 'ny stock in anything like that. Sounds to me like sour grapes. Something that was put out by some sour old maid."

She smiled and kissed him lightly and said: "I'm a big girl, darling. Don't you think you ought to put me down now? I can well imagine what Maria must be thinking of us."

Maria, who was directly behind Elena, poked her head out at Canavan and smiled broadly, her white teeth shining in her round, brown face.

"H'llo, Maria," he said. "Cómo está?"

"Muy bien, señor," she replied. She tapped Elena on the back with a stubby, short-nailed finger, and when Elena turned her head and looked at her, the broad-hipped Mexican woman said to her: "Señora, eet is not important what Maria think. Important only is what you think."

"There y'are," Canavan said. "There's a mouthful of wisdom for you. How d'you like your kitchen, Maria?"

"She is very nice, señor."

"How about it?" Canavan asked Elena. "Like what you've seen so far?"

"Oh, yes!" she answered at once. "We should be able to do lots with this house. And I love the wide veranda, John."

"Good. Now we've got to arrange with somebody to haul your furniture and stuff out here from Truxton."

"It's here already. Didn't you notice those four big wagons, freighters I think they call them, out front?"

"Didn't come that way. Came in 'round the back."

"Oh!" she said as he gently put her down. As he watched, she smoothed down the hiked-up front of her dress and moved practiced hands over her hips too, completing the smoothing down process. Then lifting her eyes to him, she said: "A new freighter, a man named Westervelt, moved into Truxton. As soon as I heard about him, I went around to see him, made a deal with him, and he and his men packed for us, loaded everything aboard his wagons, and followed us out here."

"Uh-huh. And what'd you do about the house?"

She dimpled and answered: "Sold it to another newcomer to Truxton, a lawyer named Brownlee."

He smiled a little wanly and said: "Gotta hand it to you, lady. You know what to do and how to do it and you go ahead and do it. Don't leave much for me to do for you."

"That's where you're wrong, John," she said quietly. "What you've got to do is far more important than anything I've done. I don't know anything about ranching. You do. Because I have such complete faith in you and in your judgment, I left it to you to decide whether we should buy this place or look elsewhere. And since we've bought it, I'm satisfied that you must have considered it a worthwhile buy

47

because from it you're going to make a living for us. In addition—"

"Excuse me," a voice said from behind them. Both turned their heads. Standing just outside the open doorway was Tom Bannon. "Sheriff's here to see you, boss," he said to Canavan. "Looks kinda put out about something."

Canavan frowned and said: "That old goat is getting in my hair. Looks like I'm gonna have t'do something about him." Over his shoulder he said to Elena: "Be right back."

He followed Bannon around the house, down the path to the front of it, to where Peaseley, looking both annoyed and angry, was sitting his horse. Beyond the sheriff were four huge freighters with four of the weariest-looking horses that Canavan had ever seen idling in each wagon's traces. Canvas tarpaulins were draped over the freighters' loads and secured by tightly drawn long lengths of strong rope that were pulled through iron rings at the sides of the wagons and through other rings at the back of each, and then slip-knotted. A couple of rolled-up rugs that lay at the very bottom of the nearest freighter stuck out from beneath the wagon's canvas covering.

Peaseley lost no time making known the reasons for his unexpected appearance.

"Wouldn't take my advice, huh, when I told you not to bring your family out here?" he sputtered and began to redden. "And those mavericks sittin' on the corral rail. Who are they and what are they doin' here?"

Canavan eased his hat up from his forehead and let it ride on the back of his head. Proof that it was a little snug for him was the pencil-thin red line that it left on his forehead, particularly around the temples. Mechanically he rubbed his forehead with the back of his hand, smudging it.

"Not that it's any of your business who they are, Peaseley," Canavan replied. "But I'll tell you anyway. They're my crew. And now that you've asked your question and you've got your answer, just turn yourself around and start riding. I'm kinda fussy about who I invite to come visiting."

"You're forgetting something, mister," the sheriff flared back at him. "I'm the law 'round these parts and that gives me the right to go anywhere I like. And I don't have to ask anybody's permission. Nobody comes into Indian Head and stays put without being passed on by us. This is still our town, not yours, so we have the right to say who's welcome and who isn't. Now in that scurvy-lookin' bunch hangin' around the corral, I noticed a tall, kinda dark-faced feller, and right away it came to me that there's something awf'lly f'miliar about him. I've seen him before, or—"

"For your information, Mister Sheriff," Bannon said evenly, "that tall, kinda dark-faced feller happens to be Scotty Mac-Naughton. He's been riding for me for over nine years now. So I know just about everything there is to know about him, and I can vouch for him."

Peaseley pushed his glasses higher up on his nose and leveled a long, hard look at Bannon.

"You can, huh?" he countered sarcastically. "And who'll vouch for you?"

"Why, you—"

Bannon took a step toward the sheriff only to have Canavan put out a restraining hand and stop him in his tracks.

"Don't pay 'ny attention to anything that old goat says," Canavan told him. "He's an old flannel-mouth, and he keeps runnin' off without ever knowing what he's talking about."

Hard-eyed and tight-mouthed, Bannon subsided, but he did so reluctantly, and made no attempt to conceal his resentment.

Pretending that he hadn't heard Canavan, although his deeply crimsoned face belied his attempted pretense, Peaseley went on with: "Like I said, I've seen that feller before. Or I've seen his picture, and chances are that's how I come to reco'nize him, from his picture on a poster that I've got hangin' in my office. When I get back there, I'll have a good look at it, and if I still think it's him, I'll be back for him. And just in case you think you c'n stop me from takin' him in, I'll bring a posse with me. And while I'm checkin' up on that feller, I'll do a little lookin' up on the others with him. I wouldn't be surprised if there's a want out for every one o' them too." He wheeled around, stopped and looked back at Canavan over his sloped shoulder, and said: "Told you, didn't I, that you wouldn't be able to hire any hands to ride for you? 'Course I should've expected that when you couldn't find any decent kind o' men willing to work for you, you'd wind up with the other kind, those hightailin' it from the law. But you having been a lawman once, I didn't think you'd go for the wrong kind. I'm beginning to wonder what kind of a lawman you really were. One thing I'm sure of, and that's what Stonebridge said about you was a lotta hogwash. Look for me to be back, mister, and just you try to stop me from takin' anybody I come after."

He jerked himself around, and rode away.

SIX

Suddenly aware of someone standing a bare half-step behind him, and about the same distance to the side of him, Canavan turned his head. It was Elena who was standing there.

"Oh," he said. "Didn't know you'd come out."

Then he saw the troubled look in her face.

"If I said he doesn't like you, that would be an understatement, wouldn't it?"

"Who's that? Oh, y'mean the sheriff?"

"Yes."

"I don't like him either. So that makes us even. But he doesn't worry me. Annoys me more'n anything else. I tangled

"I won't need a list if you'll let me go with you."

with his boss, Had Voight, who runs the town, and because I wouldn't go along with what he wanted, between them they fixed things up so that none of the storekeepers will do business with me. They think that by making things tough for me, they c'n force me to knuckle down to Voight and let him walk all over me, or get me so disgusted that I'll sell out and move on so's somebody else who'll kowtow to Voight can move in. Now you oughta know how far they'll get with that with me. And now that I've decided that they've gone far enough, I'm ready to do something about them. There isn't as much as a crumb to eat here. So I'd like you to get up a list of things that we oughta have and I'll go get th'm. Got a lot o' mouths to feed around here now, y'know. How about it?"

"But if the storekeepers won't sell you . . . ?"

"Kinda think I can change their minds for th'm."

"I won't need a list if you'll let me go with you."

"All right. You came in that rig of yours, didn't you?"

She nodded and said: "It's standing in front of the barn."

"Oh, yeah," he said shortly, after turning his gaze in the direction of the towering barn. "Bannon..."

Bannon had been sauntering about aimlessly, venting his feelings by kicking up tiny clods of dirt. He stopped and looked at Canavan.

"Elena and I are going into town. Gotta do some stocking up on grub and things. Nothing much for you to do here just yet 'cept get that Westervelt feller and his men started moving the furniture into the house. Maria's inside, and she can tell them where the stuff goes."

"Right, boss."

Canavan made a wry face.

"Make it John or Johnny. Anything but 'boss.'"

"Whatever you say. Only I wonder if it wouldn't be a mite smarter if I kinda trailed along with you two just in case you run into something that two guns c'n handle better'n just one. I couldn't help hearing what you were telling Elena. So I don't think you oughta try going it alone. Now don't get me wrong, boss. I mean Johnny. I know doggoned well you can take good care o' yourself. You wouldn't be alive today if you couldn't. But if those buzzards mean business and they're really fixin' to get you, having me around to kinda back your play, whatever you might decide to make it—"

Canavan, with a thin little smile parting his lips, nodded and said, interrupting him: "All right, Bannon. Go get your horse, and while you're at it, you might as well get mine too, and meet us down at the barn. C'mon, honey."

Bannon, hitching up his levis, strode briskly up the path to the rear of the house. Canavan, with Elena at his side, stopped twice before going on to the barn, the first time to tell Westervelt to start unloading the wagons and move the furniture inside; the second time, to let his new hands know that they would have to be on their own for the next couple of hours. Of course, he added, if any of them felt that they should be doing something to while away the time that they might find weighing heavily on their hands, he doubted that Westervelt's men would object if they offered their help.

As they walked on after that, hand-in-hand, Elena, still wearing her expression of concern, asked without looking up at him: "I don't suppose the good people of Indian Head know that there is a law, even though it hasn't been enforced very often, on the statute books that says that no storekeeper may legally refuse to sell his wares to anyone who wants to buy them and who has the money to pay for them?"

"No-o, I don't suppose they do know of it. But even if they did, and I'm sure that Voight does, they wouldn't dare do anything to antagonize him, he's got them so . . . so thoroughly cowed."

"Yet you think you can get them to disobey him and do as you want them to."

"That's right," he answered. He smiled a little and added: "Let's say I'll use my powers of persuasion on them. I think I can get them to see the error of their ways."

She met his eyes for a moment, then let hers fall before his and glanced at the gun that rode low-slung and tied down on his right thigh. There was no need for him to tell her how he proposed to persuade the storekeepers. It was the gun that would bring about their compliance with his demands. It was a violent country, the one in which they lived, and while she detested violence, she had to admit that all too often it was a show of force and sometimes the use of it that made peaceful living possible. She conceded too that while the Bible was probably right in its assertion that the meek would one day inherit the earth, it would not be of their doing that they would survive. It would be because of the few who were strong, who made life safe for others by daring to oppose those who sought to impose their will upon the ones who lacked the courage to fight against oppression. She knew what it meant to be tied to a weak man. Four years of married life with Gerald Blanchard hadn't left her with any happy memories. But the four years that followed his death when she had had to stand alone in a world in which men predominated strengthened her resolve that if she ever married again it would not be to another Gerald Blanchard. Now it was a month since her marriage to Canavan, and he was everything that Blanchard hadn't been. She was happy beyond belief, and she could not remember when she had felt so secure. She no longer tried to reconcile her abhorrence of violence with the fact that she gloried in his being a fighter. She could feel the steely strength in his whole being in the mere touch of his hand, and she felt strengthened by it, and her expression of concern vanished. Indian Head, she told herself, had never known anyone like her man. Its people, and that included the sheriff and the man, whatever his name was, who ran the town, had a lot to learn, and learn they would, and John Canavan would be their teacher.

She squeezed his hand and lifted her eyes to him and he smiled at her and said simply: "I'm glad you're here."

"Mean you missed me?"

"More'n you'll ever know."

"And I missed you too."

He made no response to that. But the look in his eyes told her more than anything he could have said.

She seated herself in the buggy and tucked in her full skirt around her legs while Canavan stood by patiently waiting to hand her the reins. Bannon, astride his own horse and leading the mare, came trotting up to them. A minute later, with Elena leading the way and Canavan and Bannon directly behind her, they went down the incline to the roadway. Then with the two men separating and taking up flanking positions around the buggy, they headed for town.

There was little said during the forty-minute ride to Indian Head. Bannon was the first to break the silence when he announced that it was going to be a hot day. Then a little later on it was Canavan's turn.

"When we hit town we'll pull up in front of the bank and let Elena stop in to see Stonebridge. We'll go on, you and me, Bannon, and have us a little talk with that mouthy sheriff. Think we'd better get him to understand that we don't aim to play games with him any longer, that from now on every time he bothers us he's gonna get it good. I've had more'n enough of him, and I kinda think you c'n do without any more of him too, Bannon."

"And how I can," the latter answered.

Bathed in bright, dazzling sunshine and gripped by stifling heat, Indian Head showed few signs of activity. There was hardly more than a handful of people in the street, and almost all of them were women with scarfs or shawls draped over their heads to protect them from the blazing sun and with marketing baskets swinging from their wrists or hands. There were two men too, old and shabbily dressed. But they turned into an alley and disappeared from view. The women walked as close to the buildings as they could in order to take advantage of the thin shade that they cast off. They showed little interest in anything around them, and hurried on, plainly anxious to get out of the sun's reach and into the comparative comfort of their homes. So none of the passersby noticed the rig, the woman who was driving it, or the two horsemen who accompanied her. Only a single storekeeper on the opposite side of the street who was standing well back of the open doorway of his establishment glimpsed the trio as they halted diagonally across the way from him in front of the bank. Resentful of the sun's interference with his business, he was much too annoyed with the elements to do anything more than glance mechanically at the strangers. After another moment he turned on his heel and trudged back into the shadowy depths of his store.

Canavan swung down from the mare, patted her sweat-matted rump, and stepped up on the walk. He waited at the side of the buggy till Elena wound the reins around the handbrake, stood up, and moved toward Canavan. Carefully he lifted her over the left front wheel, turned with her, and set her down lightly on the walk.

"Where will you be when I come out?" she wanted to know of him.

"If you get finished visiting with Stonebridge and we're not out here waiting for you, go back inside and wait. No point in you standing around in the street in all this heat. When we get done with our business with Peaseley, we'll come back for you. All right?"

She nodded and started across the walk, then stopped within a couple of steps of the bank door, and looked back at him as though she were about to say something, perhaps to caution him to be careful. Apparently she reconsidered; she turned abruptly and went swiftly into the bank.

Canavan and Bannon rode on down the deserted street till they came to the sheriff's office. They pulled up at the low curb and dismounted, tied up their horses at the hitchrail in front of the place, and with Canavan striding ahead of Bannon, trooped inside. When Canavan gestured, Bannon closed the door and backed against it and stood slightly spread-legged with his hands on his hips.

Peaseley, bareheaded this time, his thinning hair mussed, was sitting behind his desk. A batch of posters was spread out over the desk before him. On a small table behind him was an uneven pile of posters that was topped by his hat. He sat back and stared up at them open-mouthed, an indication of his surprise at seeing them. He swallowed hard, his Adam's apple jerking convulsively for a brief moment.

"What . . . what are fellers doing here?" he wheezed.

Canavan sauntered up to the desk, sniffed loudly a couple of times, and made a wry face.

"Stinks in here," he said. "Don't you ever air out this place?"

"Maybe the stink's coming from him," Bannon said. "Bet he doesn't remember the last time he had a bath."

Peaseley, bristling with indignation, leaped up from his chair.

"Now just one goldarned minute," he sputtered, his face crimsoning. Angrily he shoved his spectacles higher up on his nose. But they didn't stay there very long; in fact, they slid right down again. Shaking a crooked finger at Bannon, he said: "I'm the law around here, and if you don't wanna wind up behind bars, you'd better show some respect."

Canavan took off his hat, hauled out his bandana, mopped his head and face with it and wiped the sweatband dry, pocketed the bandana, and put on his hat. He said simply: "Show me that picture you were talking about."

"I don't hafta show you anything!"

"He's had another look at it, Johnny, and he knows damned well it isn't Scotty," Bannon said.

"I know that. But I'd still like to see it."

"So would I. Just for the hell of it. How about it, Peaseley?"

Crowding the spread-out posters together into a single pile, the flushed sheriff covered it with both hands. He looked up defiantly and said: "I'm not showing you anything because I don't hafta. Now you two get outta here."

"You say the word, Johnny," Bannon said, balling up his right fist and grinding it into the palm of his left hand, "and I'll wallop that mis'rable old bastid good. I don't like his tongue or his face, but I can't do anything about his tongue 'cept cut it out of him, and that's a helluva job to have t'do, messy as all get-out, 'less you've got a good sharp knife, and I haven't. Mine's kinda dull, and I'd have to hack away at him with it and cut out a lotta little hunks till I got it all out of him. Be a helluva lot easier to give him a good walloping. Dunno that it would improve his looks any. But I'd kinda concentrate on that big mouth of his and maybe I could close it for him for good. What do you say, John?"

The color had drained out of Ab Peaseley's face and now it was a sickish grayish-white. He drew back in his chair, with his eyes wide with fear and tiny beads of sweat dotting his forehead, and pushed back even farther when Bannon took a step toward him.

"You—you lay a hand on me and you'll see what'll happen to you," he wheezed.

"No, Bannon," Canavan said, waving the former back. "We don't want to soil our hands on him. He isn't worth it."

Bannon looked disappointed. He backed again to the door.

Canavan looked hard at the sheriff, and leaning over the desk, said to him: "Gonna tell you this for the last time, Peaseley. Stay the hell out of my way. And stay away from my crew and the O-Bar. I won't tell you what I'll do to you if you don't. All I'll tell you is that you'll get it good. Now you remember that." Settling his hat more securely on his head, and turning to Bannon, he said: "All right, Tom. Let's go."

Bannon opened the door and held it wide, and followed Canavan out to the street. He stopped and reached for the doorknob, curled his hand around it, and yanked the door shut with such force that it nearly came unhinged. The dirt-smudged oblong piece of glass in the middle of the upper panel fell in with a shattering crash that brought a howl of protest from inside the office. Bannon and Canavan looked at each other and exchanged a grin.

Take our horses or d'we leave 'em here for now?" Bannon asked.

"Leave 'em," Canavan replied. "Every time that old goat in there looks out, he'll see th'm, and they'll remind him of us. He won't like it. But there isn't anything he can do about it. He's been getting under my skin ever since I got here. Let's get under his skin for a change."

"I'm for that," Bannon responded.

They marched up the street. As they neared the bank, Elena emerged, stopped when she saw them coming, and waited.

When they came up to her she said: "John, Mr. Stonebridge asked me to tell you how grateful he is for what you did for him." Then with a little smile playing around her mouth, she added: "You forgot to tell me about that, didn't you, darling? Of course, thwarting a bank robbery isn't very important. So I can understand why it slipped your mind. And there were some other things that you were involved in here, weren't there? But they weren't important either, were they?"

"Nope, not to us," he answered calmly. "They were maybe a mite important at the minute that they happened. But not after that. Anyway, long's I remember to tell you about things that are important to us . . ."

She smiled again and said: "Of course."

He took her by the arm and started to cross the street with her. Tom Bannon moved behind her and came up alongside of her and took her other arm.

She said: "Mr. Stonebridge suggested that we try Floyd Thayer's general store, the Emporium. He said they have just about everything we might want, from, well, foodstuffs to, well, you name it and more than likely they have it."

"Uh-huh," Canavan said as they mounted the opposite curb. "The Emporium's the place I was planning to take you."

The big sign above the double windows had lost some of the color that backgrounded the words THE EMPORIUM, but the letters were still plainly visible and easily readable. Bannon followed them into the store and halted just inside the open doorway with his thumbs stuck in his belt, while Elena, with Canavan a step behind her, walked to the long wooden counter that right-angled the windows. Standing at it was a back-turned woman who was studying what appeared to be an envelope that held a rather long list of pencil-written items. As Elena came up to the counter, the woman took her eyes

56

from the list, turned her head and smiled at Elena. She said: "Floyd will be right back. He's just gone downstairs to get me something from the cellar."

"Thank you," Elena responded.

The woman, an attractive brunette of about forty, neatly and becomingly dressed, lifted her gaze to Canavan, who had just come up alongside of Elena, and said to him: "You're that awful Canavan man, aren't you?"

Instinctively Elena bristled, and just as she was about to snap back at the woman, Canavan said: " 'Fraid so, ma'am."

So Elena held her tongue.

"I thought so," the woman continued. "I was told you're redheaded and big, and you are indeed. But you don't look particularly frightening to me. I've seen any number of men, smaller than you by far, who were really vicious looking." Then in somewhat of a musing tone she added: "So you've already had the doubtful pleasure of meeting my son and his father."

"Then you must be Addie Voight."

"That's right. I'm Paulie's mother, and while I'm still legally bound to his father, we parted company a long time ago. One of these days, though, I'll get around to divorcing him, and that will be that." She paused as though she expected him to make some kind of comment. When he offered none, she went on with: "You're one of the few men around here who's had the courage to stand up to Had. I hope it doesn't lead to trouble for you. As for Paulie, he isn't really bad or mean. Thank goodness he didn't inherit his father's vindictiveness. It's just that in common with a lot of others of Paulie's age, he too became obsessed with the notion that the most important thing in a man's life is to be a fast gun. I don't know if what you did to him has taught him anything, if he realizes how foolish the idea is. I don't know because he refuses to talk about it. I'm told you could have killed him had you wanted to. But you didn't, and I'm grateful to you for sparing him." Her gaze returned to Elena. "You're very pretty, Mrs. Canavan. Oh, you are Mrs. Canavan, aren't you?"

Elena smiled and said quite simply: "Yes, I am."

All three turned their heads and looked toward the shadowy rear of the store when they heard approaching footsteps coming from that direction.

Addie said: "Here comes Floyd now."

He was a middle-aged, average-sized, aproned man with thinning hair carefully combed and plastered down over a wide expanse of pinkish scalp in an effort to conceal his baldness. He moved behind the counter and said to the Voight woman: "Couldn't remember if I had 'ny left, Addie. That's why I had to go take a look. How many did you say you wanted?"

"Six, if you have that many."

"Six is what I've got. I'll send th'm over with the other things."

Eyeing him, Canavan was struck by the curious resemblance that the man bore to Had Voight even though he was a Thayer instead of a Voight.

"Musta been a lot o' intermarriage between the two families," he thought to himself.

Floyd looked at Elena, raised his eyes to Canavan, flushed a little under the eyes, and said with a shake of his head: "Sorry, mister. But I'll have to ask you to take your business somewhere else."

"You wanna tell him about the law?" Canavan asked Elena. "If you don't wanna be bothered, it'll be all right with me. I'd just as soon heave him through that window as not. I don't like the Thayers any more than I do the Voights."

"Please, John," she answered, and half-turning, said to the storekeeper: "Apparently you aren't aware of this, Mr. Thayer. But the law forbids you to discriminate for any reason whatsoever. I'm a lawyer, so I know. In other words, you cannot refuse to sell anyone who wants to buy what you have to sell as long as that person has the money with which to pay you. That, Mr. Thayer, is the law. Now what you choose to do about it, obey it or disobey it, is up to you."

"I don't understand, Floyd," Addie said. "Why don't you want to sell them? Business isn't that good that you can afford to turn it away when it's offered to you."

"I can tell you why he doesn't want to deal with us," Canavan said, and Addie looked at him. "Had's sent that pussyfooting sheriff of his around to all the storekeepers to tell them that he doesn't want any of th'm to sell us anything."

"Oh, so that's it! So Had's still playing God, is he?"

No one answered. Hitching up his belt, Canavan stepped around Elena so that he stood between her and Addie Voight and squarely across the counter from the storekeeper.

"When you get finished seein' to what Mrs. Voight wants," he said evenly to Thayer, "my wife'll tell you what she wants, and if you know what's good for you, mister, you'll be nice about it and you'll take care of her same's you would one o' your own folks. I'm kinda fussy 'bout the way people treat my wife, so you'd better watch it. Understand? Now get along with what you're doing for Mrs. Voight. She hasn't got all day and neither have we."

"He has my order," Addie said. "So he's free to take care of you now, Mrs. Canavan."

"Thank you," Elena said.

Addie smiled at her, and as she turned to go, Canavan touched his hat to her. As she walked to the door and neared Bannon, he straightened up, and as Canavan had done, touched his hat to her. She gave him a smile and went out.

"Kinda think you oughta double up on everything that you were gonna get," Canavan suggested to Elena.

She nodded understandingly.

"Yes, I think I should too."

Floyd Thayer raised his eyes to her.

"Whenever you're ready, ma'am," he said.

SEVEN

The Canavan order was one of the largest that Floyd Thayer had been called upon to fill in a long time. Under ordinary conditions, and if the customer had been someone else, the thought of being able to move so much of his stock that had been doing nothing save occupy space, and a quick figuring in his mind of the profit that would result from the sale, would have delighted him. But all he could think of was Had Voight, and that overshadowed everything else. Mindful of what had happened to others who hadn't followed Had's dictates to the letter, he knew what to expect when Had learned that he had made a sale to the undesirable and unwanted Canavan.

Had would come storming in and he would light into him, and the tongue-lashing that he would unleash made Floyd feel sick in anticipation of it. Had wouldn't give him a chance to say anything in his own defense. He would do all the talking, and very likely a lot of yelling too, for that was characteristic of Had, and when he was finished, he would simply turn on his heel and stalk out. Still thinking of what he had been told, Floyd would feel like a whipped dog when Had finished with him; his ears would burn and ring for hours after, and his head would throb so violently that he would close his eyes and keep them closed for fear that opening them might induce his head to burst. Finally, he would grope his way blindly to some dark, out-of-the-way corner, turn and back himself into it, and then collapse in it. If that happened to him, after a while when the ringing began to abate and the throbbing showed signs of lessening, and he was able to force himself up into a sitting position without suffering any reaction to movement, he wouldn't let it end there. As soon as he felt equal to facing Had again, he would seek him out, and even if he had to hold a gun on Had to make him hold still and listen, he would tell him that what he had done he would do all over again if he had to choose between disobeying Had and incurring his displeasure and letting Canavan force him into submission. He had heard enough about the big, broad-shouldered, redheaded man to know that he was not the kind whom anyone in his right mind would try to deny anything he wanted. He would explain that he had had no reason to doubt that Canavan would have done exactly as he had said he would, heave him through his own window, if he, Floyd, had refused to fill Mrs. Canavan's order. So it had left him with no alternative but to obey the big man. He wouldn't tell Had that the thought of being picked up like a bag of meal and thrown through his window had made him shudder, and that thinking about it now made him shudder all over again.

Only if Had rejected his explanation and refused to hear any more from him would he remind Had that he hadn't done so well when he had tried to overawe and intimidate Canavan, and that Had's son Paulie had wound up with a bullet in his shoulder as a result of his one brief encounter with Canavan. And if that wasn't enough, he would remind Had of Curly Simmons, and of what had happened to the foolish youth when he took it upon himself to square accounts with Canavan for Paulie, Tommy Thayer, and himself by attempting to potshot Canavan. Curly missed when he shouldn't have, Floyd would say. But Canavan hadn't missed. His bullet had found its mark. So the youth was dead.

Thinking of those things made Floyd feel better. But when he tried to picture himself facing down Had and forcing him to hear him out, he had to admit that he doubted he would ever have the courage to go through with it. So, gloomily thinking his disappointing thoughts, he set about attending to Elena's wants.

When he heard the first two items, six full-sized sacks of potatoes and three barrels of flour, he winced inwardly. The first weighed about one hundred pounds each; the barrels of flour, about one hundred and fifty pounds each. Since the potatoes were stored in the cellar, and since he could only carry one sack at a time, six sacks meant six trips down the rickety stairs and six up. Each sack seemed to be heavier than the one before. By the time he came staggering up the stairs with the last sack draped over his sagging shoulder, he was spent and wheezing. He had to rest a bit before he felt able to go on assembling the things Elena wanted.

The flour in bulk was kept in the storeroom at the far rear of the Emporium. Heavily Floyd trudged off to get it. Again it was a one-at-a-time procedure, dragging the nearest barrel to the door, maneuvering the barrel and himself through the door, then tilting it and wheeling it rather than simply rolling it forward to where he had dumped the sacks of potatoes. He was exhausted when he returned with the third barrel, so completely spent that despite his efforts to let it down gently on the floor, it came down with such a crash that the whole building seemed to rise up off its foundation. Slowly it settled itself again, and so too did the thin cloud of dust that had boiled up from the floor around the barrel.

Fortunately for Floyd, most of the other items that Elena ordered were far lighter in weight and closer at hand. When he had gotten everything together, he breathed a deep sigh of relief. He was soaked with perspiration and his shirt clung to him so tightly he had difficulty pulling it away from his body. When he picked up a couple of stubs of pencils, selected one and put down the others, and started to list the prices on a paper bag, his hand trembled so from his exertions, he had to turn over the job to Elena.

When it was finished and Elena returned the bag to him so that he could total it, Canavan asked: "How about some things that I want?"

Turning his head and lifting his eyes to him, Thayer asked: "Like what?"

"Like six bunk mattresses, a whole mess of fence wire, couple of gallons o' red paint, couple o' white, say four or five brushes, couple o' wire cutters, couple o' small buckets and a couple o' large ones, and a toolbox, and you'd better fill it up with whatever you think it oughta have. 'Less of course, you've got one already made up. Oh-h, and I'm gonna need a couple o' branding irons. Can you have them made up for me? Do I have to order 'em from—?"

"I can take care of them for you," the storekeeper said, interrupting him. "Gonna keep using the O-Bar-O brand, or you got your own?"

"We'll use our own," Canavan replied. "The JC."

"Mr. Thayer," Elena said. "I forgot a couple of brooms."

He smiled a little wearily and nodded.

"I'll get 'em," he said, putting the paper bag and the pencil stub on the counter. Turning again to Canavan, he asked: "You got a wagon or something to haul all this stuff away in out to your place?"

"No, not yet. While you're getting the things I want and my wife's brooms, I'm going up the street to the stable and see if I can make a deal for a wagon and a team of horses."

"John," Elena said. "When you come back, can we get some breakfast? I'm starved."

Canavan rubbed his chin thoughtfully with the back of his hand.

"Need a shave," he said as though to himself. Then to Elena: "There's a lunchroom. But it isn't much of a place, and the food isn't anything to write home about."

"S'matter with Addie's?" Thayer asked.

"Hey, that's right. Forgot about her."

"She runs a nice, clean place," Thayer continued, "and you can't beat her cooking. Serves only the best. I know because she gets everything she uses from me, and I don't take in anything that isn't the best. Right down the street, y'know, on the other side."

"I know," Canavan said to him, then to Elena: "I'll make it as quick as I can."

As Thayer trudged off to the rear to get the brooms for Elena, Canavan started for the door only to stop in his tracks, and frown. Through the wide open door he could see two men, Had Voight and Ab Peaseley, coming across the street. Had wore an angry look, and Canavan sensed that it had something to do with him. Bannon, noticing the deepening frown on Canavan's face, poked his head out cautiously, and stole a quick, guarded look outside; when he saw the two men, the sheriff a bare half-step behind Voight, mount the curb and come across the walk to the Emporium, he hastily withdrew his head, backed off a bit, and waited with his hand resting on the butt of his gun.

Backing to Elena's side, Canavan said low-voiced to her: "We're getting company. Had Voight and that pussyfooting shadow of his, the sheriff. But it's all right. Nothing to get alarmed over."

Despite her resolve not to look, her head turned anyway, and she glanced doorward. Voight and the foot-dragging Peaseley, with the latter now a full step behind Had, came into the store. When Voight stopped and eyed the huge pile of things that Floyd Thayer had already assembled for the Canavans, with the three barrels of flour standing resolutely in the middle of the pile and the sacks of potatoes leaning against them and ringing them, and with other items of foodstuffs heaped high on top of the barrels, the none-too-alert Peaseley crowded into Had and trampled him. Scowling, Voight pushed him off with a backward sweep of his right arm. Raising his gaze, and deliberately avoiding looking at Canavan, he waited till Thayer, carrying two brooms, returned from the rear. The storekeeper, seeing him, paled.

"What is all this, Floyd?" Had demanded with a wave of his hand in the general direction of the piled-up merchandise. "Who's it for?"

Thayer, still clutching the two brooms, and his face a grayish-white, gulped and swallowed hard. Apparently it was a painful thing to do for he grimaced. When he tried to answer, he almost choked. So all he could do was indicate Canavan with a jerk of his head.

"Ab told you you weren't to sell him anything, didn't he?" Had demanded.

"Told him same's I told all the others," Peaseley said.

"I'll talk to you about this later on," Voight said curtly to Thayer. "Meantime put it all back where it came from." Then leveling a full look at Canavan, Had said coldly: "You can't buy anything in this or any other store in Indian Head. So get out."

Canavan did not answer.

"And if that woman's with you, get her out of here too."

Canavan smiled thinly and said: "That woman happens to be my wife."

"I don't give a damn who she is," Voight retorted. "Just get her out of here and be quick about it." When neither of the Canavans moved, he lost his temper. His normally swarthy face turned livid, and he yelled: "Get out, I said! Get out!"

Ignoring him, Canavan turned to Floyd Thayer, who was still pasty-faced and who had been shuttling his troubled eyes from one to the other, and said to him: "Get the rest of our stuff."

"Aw, now look, mister," the storekeeper began protestingly. "You wanna make more trouble for me than you have already?"

Had lunged suddenly, not at Canavan but at Elena. He made a grab for her wrist, obviously to drag her away from the counter. But she was too quick for him. She pulled back out of reach.

"Why, you—!" Canavan said, recovering from his surprise.

He lashed out at Voight with his left hand and cuffed him viciously in the face, staggering him back. When he saw Had go for his gun, he swarmed over him. His big balled-up fist exploded in Had's already reddened face with such pulverizing force that his hat flew off and fluttered away while Had, half-flung around, fell against the counter, caromed off it, and slid down to the floor on his backside. He slumped over on his face, and lay there. Peaseley was so stunned that he stood rooted to the floor and stared wide-eyed and open-mouthed at the motionless Voight. Suddenly, though, he snapped his mouth shut, and stepping back, went for his hip-worn gun.

Apparently Peaseley hadn't noticed Bannon in there before. So he was taken even more completely by surprise than Canavan had been by Had when Bannon came up swiftly

64

behind him, tore the half-drawn gun out of his hand, and flung it away. Then, getting a firm grip on the sheriff's frayed shirt collar with his left hand and grabbing a fistful of the shiny seat of his thin-worn pants in his right hand, Bannon swung him around. Using his right knee as a propellant, Bannon herded him across the floor to the open doorway, and with a mighty heave, threw him out. Peaseley landed on the walk on his hands and knees, and unable to stop himself, sprawled across the planks on his face and right shoulder.

Because he was dazed, it took the sheriff a minute before he was able to haul himself up on his feet. Turning himself around, he stumbled back into the doorway, leaned against the framework for another moment, and shaking a crooked, trembling finger at Bannon, wheezed breathlessly: "All right, mister. Next time I see you, I'm takin' you in. If you think you c'n manhandle the law and get away with it, you've got another think coming."

Voight stirred and forced himself up into a sitting position. His face was bloodied, and the left side of it looked strangely yellowish. There was a dazed, glassy look in his eyes. When he struggled to get up, it proved too much for him and he sank down again. Bannon bent over him and hauled him up to his feet; briefly, Had clung to Bannon's arm. Then he suddenly pushed Bannon away, and after making a futile attempt to straighten up, staggered out to the doorway where the sheriff, obviously all right again, grabbed him and steadied him and led him out of the store.

Bannon scooped up Voight's hat and scaled it away after them. It soared over their heads and dropped in the gutter a couple of feet ahead of them. Standing a little spread-legged in the doorway and following them with his eyes, Bannon saw them stop when they came to where it lay flat on its brim in the churned-up dirt. The sheriff bent over and picked it up, eyed it, and beat it vigorously a couple of times against his leg, then clapped it on Had's head only to have the latter promptly snatch it off, turn it around, and put it on himself. A moment later they were stepping up on the opposite curb. Now, Bannon noticed, Voight was walking unaided.

Suddenly Bannon became aware of the presence of a handful of spectators across the street. Just as he did, they too turned their heads and watched Had and Peaseley trudge down the street. When the onlookers saw the two men enter the sheriff's office and close the door behind them, they turned slowly and sauntered away. But one man returned, came trudging across the street, and despite the fact that Bannon was blocking the doorway, he tried to get a look inside the store. When Bannon said something to him that he did not reply to, he stepped back and tramped away.

Bannon grinned a little, backed inside, and turned around. He heard Canavan say to Elena: "Sorry that had to happen with you in the middle of it. You all right?"

"Yes, of course I am."

"He hurt your wrist?"

"No. He didn't actually touch me although it may have looked that way to you. Just barely grazed my wrist with his fingertips. I drew back too quickly for him to do any more than that. What do you think he intended to do with me, John? Drag me out of here?"

"Could be," Canavan answered. "No telling for sure, though, just what he had in mind. He got so mad and so red in the face, I thought he was gonna, well, bust a blood vessel or something."

Sauntering toward them, Bannon said: "That was quite a wallop you fetched him, Johnny. Kinda surprised me that it didn't open his face for him."

"When he fell and lay so still," Elena said, "I was afraid he was dead."

"Take him a long time to get over that wallop," Bannon added. "And all that yellow on the side of his face will be a nice black 'n blue. How about the wagon, Johnny? You gonna go see about getting it?"

"Yes, right now," Canavan said. "You stay here with Elena, Tom. Not that I expect them to come back. But just in case, y'know? Oh-h, where'd that Thayer go?"

"I'm right here," Thayer answered fairly close behind Elena, but in something of a muffled voice. He struggled into view with a paper-wrapped mattress draped over his head, shrugged it off, and stood it up on its side. He pushed it in close to the pile that had aroused Had Voight's ire, and let it lean against a couple of potato sacks. "Reckon I might as well fill the rest o' your order. Wasn't gonna at first. But then I got to thinking that Had'll have just as much to say when he gets around to it as he would've if I hadda sold you, oh-h, say a hunk o' bread. So like Addie said, and you musta heard her, business isn't that good 'round these parts that I can afford to pass up any. So . . ."

"'Course," Canavan said.

"Only one thing, mister."

"What's that?" Canavan wanted to know.

"I don't know what it'll be the next time you want something."

"Suppose we cross that bridge when we come to it?"

"Yeah, sure," Thayer said quickly.

Hitching up his belt, Canavan marched out of the store and turned upstreet. There was no one about. The heat hung just as oppressively as it had earlier, while the blazing sun's rays were even more wilting than they had been. To shield his eyes from the glare, he yanked down his hat brim as far as he could.

Ossie Blue, wearing an ankle-length apron that was doubled over at the waist because it was too long for him, was idling a step inside the doorway of his place when Canavan came striding along.

"Hey, partner, what's the rush in all this heat?" he asked. "How about coming inside where it's nice and comf'table? Besides, the beer's cold and waiting for somebody with a thirst to lap it up. First customer gets his first beer free. What d'you say?"

" 'Fraid I can't take the time for that today, Ossie. Left my wife in the Emporium, and I don't wanna keep her waiting. Some other time, huh?"

"Yeah, sure," the friendly, talkative undersized saloonkeeper answered. He stepped out on the walk and Canavan halted and eyed him questioningly. "I got a look at Had's face when he came staggering out of the Emporium," Ossie added, "and I knew right off that it couldn't have been anybody but you who coulda done that kind of a job on him. His face looked kinda pushed in, like maybe one of his steers had stepped on it. Like I said, I knew it couldn't have been anybody but you because there isn't anybody else around this flea-bitten town who has the guts to stand up to Mister Had Voight."

"He brought it on himself."

"Knowing Had the way I do, he must've."

Ossie gave Canavan a half-salute when the latter continued on his way up the street.

Some ten minutes later Bannon heard a wagon come rumbling down the street. He poked his head out, took one look, withdrew it, turned and said to Elena: "Johnny. Sure made it back quick, didn't he?"

"Did he get the wagon?"

"Yeah, sure. Looks like a good-sized one too."

"We'll need a good-sized one for all the things we've bought."

As she came forward to the door, she saw a heavy farm wagon hauled by a team of sturdy-looking horses grind to a stop at the curb in front of them. Bannon moved alongside of her. As they watched, Canavan climbed down from the wagon's wide seat, and came striding across the walk. Bannon and Elena stepped back so that he could come inside.

"Mean the stableman hadn't got word that he wasn't to sell you anything?" Bannon asked with a crooked little smile.

"Looks like it, doesn't it?" Canavan countered. "Could be that Peaseley forgot about him. Or it coulda been his boss who forgot. Or it coulda been that they were thinking only of the storekeepers. Point is, I got the wagon and the team at what I think was a pretty fair price."

"Swell," Bannon said. "No arguments, no nothing, huh?"

"And no mention of Had Voight or Peaseley. I didn't know what to expect when I went into the stable. So after that set-to with Voight and old flannel-mouth, I was awf'lly glad to find the stableman so friendly-like. Thayer finished getting our stuff together?"

Bannon nodded and said: "Uh-huh. And just waiting for us to get it outta here."

"I checked the bill, John," Elena said, "and signed it, and told Mr. Thayer to take it over to the bank and get his money from Mr. Stonebridge."

"Fine," Canavan said. "Now what d'you say, Tom, we start loading the wagon?"

"I'm ready. We'll put the big stuff in first, right?"

"Right. We'll begin with the mattresses, stand them up along the insides of the wagon, then the barrels, the sacks of potatoes, and so on. Elena . . ."

She lifted her eyes to him.

"Elena, why don't you go over to that Addie's place and have yourself some breakfast while we're clearing our stuff out of here?"

"What about your own breakfast?" Elena asked. "And what about Tom's?"

"Tell you what," Canavan said. "Have yourself some coffee and wait with the rest of your breakfast. Soon's we get finished, we'll follow you over. All right?"

Y-es, but don't forget. I'm one of those awful and unwanted Canavans, you know. So don't ride off and leave me here. If you should do that, and if that dear, droll Mr. Had Voight whose fingernails need cutting should find me here alone, goodness only knows what he might do with me. He might have me burned at the stake."

"No-o, I don't think so."

"Then he might have me tarred and feathered and ridden out of his precious Indian Head on a rail, and that would be terribly uncomfortable."

"Yeah, I imagine it would."

"Your concern and your . . . your solicitude overwhelm me."

Canavan grinned at her.

"Don't they though? But I don't think you oughta worry

your pretty head about Had. We won't leave you here. That's a promise. But if I should forget, I'm sure that Bannon here will think of it and remind me."

"H'm" she said, turned and walked to the door and stepped outside. But almost immediately she was back inside again, turning and calling: "John!"

Canavan and Bannon, each of them about to lift and shoulder a mattress, stopped and looked wonderingly at her.

"I don't think I want any breakfast after all," she said.

Canavan's mattress thumped on the floor, and Bannon's touched down almost immediately after.

"There are men with rifles in the alleys directly across the street from here," she told Canavan a little excitedly as he came to her side, "and I think they're waiting for you two to show yourselves so they can shoot you down."

EIGHT

There were quick approaching footsteps, and Floyd Thayer, looking even more troubled than he had before, came hurrying from somewhere at the rear of the store.

"My wife tells me that when she happened to look outta the window," he began somewhat out of breath, "she saw some men, oh, six or eight o' th'm, and all o' th'm carrying rifles, standing in the alleys across the street, and they seemed to be looking over here. Kinda think you've stirred up something walloping Had Voight. He ain't the kind to let something like that go by without squaring up."

"Got a back door out of here?" Canavan asked him.

"Yeah, sure."

"How about the back yards? They all cluttered up, or d'you think—?"

"Mine's a mite more crowded than the others, I suppose, being that barrels and boxes seem to fill up a yard faster'n other things do. But all in all, I wouldn't say that any o' th'm, and that includes my yard, are really bad. So you people shouldn't have too much trouble makin' your way through th'm, upstreet or down."

"Bank's about five or six doors up from here, isn't it?"

"Six," Thayer said. "But it isn't on this side o' the street, y'know. On the other side."

"I know. Tom, keep an eye on things out front but without showing yourself, understand? I wanna have a look out back."

"Right," Bannon said.

Canavan and he moved off in different directions. The former returned shortly.

70

"All clear out back," he announced. "No sign of anybody that I could see. Thayer . . ."

"Yeah?"

"I'd like you to take my wife out the back way. Then see that she reaches the alley opposite the bank. She'll go the rest of the way by herself."

The storekeeper looked both surprised and disappointed.

"Mean you fellers aren't going too? Mean you're gonna stay put here?" he asked. "Cost me two hundred dollars just a couple o' months ago to fix up this place and I wouldn't wanna have it shot up on me. That's why I was hoping when you asked me about the back door and the back yard that all three o' you were gonna clear out. But if you fellers are fixin' to stay on here, I'm afraid it'll wind up in a shoot-out, and that wouldn't be fair to me or . . . or right."

"We don't intend to bring on a shoot-out," Canavan said. "If anybody shoots up your place it'll be Had Voight's doing, and he'll be the one responsible for it. Not us. That pile o' stuff," and he indicated it with a nod, "is ours and so's that wagon outside and the team hitched to it. We don't aim to let any of it fall into Voight's hands. That's why we're staying put here. To defend ourselves and our property. What's more, we don't intend to let Had think he could make us turn tail and run. If he wants a showdown, this is as good a time for it as any. Elena . . ."

"Yes?"

"Go with him, honey. When you come up out of the alley and you hit the street, go right straight across into the bank and stay there."

"Why can't I stay here too?" Elena wanted to know. "I won't be in the way. I can find a place for myself somewhere in the back."

Canavan shook his head.

"No," he said gently but firmly. "If there's gonna be any gunplay, I don't want you around. There's always a chance of a stray shot hitting where it hadn't ought to, or a bullet ricocheting, and I'm not gonna take that chance."

"All right, John. Whatever you say."

"C'mon. I'll take you to the door and see that you get started. C'mon, Thayer."

With the unhappy-looking storekeeper leading the way and the Canavans trooping along at his run-down heels, they made their way through the shadowy rear of the store to the back door. There they stopped. Curling his big hands around Elena's arms, Canavan turned her around and brought her close to him. Discreetly Thayer turned his back on them.

"I don't want you to go worrying yourself over me,"

Canavan told Elena, low-voiced. "I've been in a lot tighter fixes than this one, believe me, and I came out of them with a whole skin. And this one doesn't even begin to compare with some of the others."

"Just be careful, please."

" 'Course I'll be careful," he assured her, and added lightly: "I've got me some plans for the future, and being that I aim to carry th'm out, I've got to be around."

He kissed her and released her. Thayer turned around.

"I keep this door open in the summertime so's I can get some air inside," he said. "Want me to close it now?"

"No. Leave it open."

"All right, ma'am," Thayer said to Elena.

He went out first, and Elena, with an over-the-shoulder glance at Canavan, followed the storekeeper. Peering out through the crack in the open door, Canavan saw them wind their way through a pile-up of boxes on one side and upended barrels on the other. Then just as they neared the adjoining yard, Canavan heard a voice call out from somewhere out of his range of vision: "H'llo, Floyd."

Thayer stopped instantly and looked back over his shoulder.

"Oh-h, h'llo, Jess . . . Walt. What are you fellers doing back here?"

"Oh, nothing special," was the reply.

"Yeah, sure," Canavan thought to himself. "Just layin' for me or Bannon. Had musta told them not to let on to Thayer that they're supposed to be guarding the back door. I'm glad I know they're here. That way I won't go stepping outside and getting myself shot up."

Lifting his gaze past Thayer for the moment, Canavan saw that Elena had walked on a bit. Now, though, she stopped and stood half-turned as she waited for Thayer to rejoin her. He did shortly, came trudging up to Elena, and walked on with her. He stepped ahead of her once to lift and hold high a sagging washline so that she could pass under it without having to bend. Canavan heard approaching scuffing boot-steps, and presently two rifle-armed men came sauntering along and halted just beyond the open door.

"I was afraid you were gonna say something more to Floyd," one of the men said to his companion, "so's he'd know what we're doing here."

"You ever know me to run off at the mouth?"

"No-o, can't say that I do, Jess. I'm wondering, though, if it wouldn't've been even better if we hadda ducked outta sight when we saw Floyd come out, instead o' letting him see us."

"Forget it, Walt. He won't think anything. Floyd isn't a

72

bad sort. But he's about as dumb as anybody I've ever laid eyes on. So I'll bet you he's satisfied with what I told him."

"All the same, I think we oughta duck outta sight till after he comes back. Dumb or no, I don't think we oughta go giving him ideas."

"All right, Walt. I'm kinda curious about him and that woman. She was a right good looker, and a stranger to boot. Now where d'you suppose he was taking her?"

"I wouldn't know. What's more, I couldn't care less. You gonna stand here, or you gonna do like I—"

"Gimme another minute. I can still see them. I wanna see where they go. Then we'll go back down the alley."

Apparently satisfied, the man named Walt did not press him again. Instead he asked rather musingly: "Wonder what Lily'd have to say if she saw Floyd gallivanting around the back yards with another woman, and a kinda nice looking one like that one?"

Jess snorted and half-turned to him.

"You hafta wonder?" he demanded. "Mean you don't know? Hell, she'd pin his ears back for him. That woman's got a mouth on her and a tongue to match. My Hannah can do a pretty good job on a man once she sets her mind to it. But that Lily Thayer can just about cut a man to pieces with that tongue of hers."

"I know. I've heard her let loose a couple o' times."

"Yeah? And what'd she sound like?"

"Well, all I can tell you is that I was awf'lly glad it wasn't me she'd lit into. I can't see them now, Jess. So what do you say we drift back to that alley? After Floyd gets back we can slip out again and cover the door from close up. Huh?"

A little reluctantly, it seemed to Canavan, Jess turned.

"Wonder if those two buzzards in there," he said with a nod at the open door, "have any idea what Had's got set up for them?"

Before Walt answered, he glanced at the door. "Don't look like it to me," he said. "Or they'd've tried to make a break for it, wouldn't they?"

"Didn't somebody say he thought he saw a woman start to come out and then back inside again?"

"Yeah, only I kinda forget who it was who said it. But that doesn't prove anything. Coulda been Lily or somebody else who decided it was too blamed hot outside and changed her mind and stayed put."

"Wonder if it coulda been that woman with Floyd? If it was . . ."

"Yeah?"

". . . and she spotted the bunch of us across the street and figured that something was gonna happen and decided it would be safer for her to get outta there while the getting was still good, but out the back way instead o' the front way, she coulda tipped off that Canavan feller and his side-partner. Right?"

"Yeah, she coulda. And if she did, how come they haven't made a break for it?"

Obviously Jess had no ready answer for him. So he simply grunted and said: "C'mon."

As the two men moved past the back door to return to the far-side alley from which they had been watching the door, Canavan moved too. His gun flashed in his hand as he spun out from behind the door. He glided noiselessly over the ground-into-the-earth threshold strip, and came up behind the unsuspecting Jess and Walt just as silently.

"Hold it," he commanded, and poked one in the back, then the other, with his gun. "All right. Drop those rifles and reach."

Jess obeyed without any further urging or prodding, dropped his rifle in the dirt and pushed it away from him with his boot-toe. Walt delayed, and obeyed only when the hard, uncompromising muzzle of Canavan's Colt collided with his spine, making him wince. His rifle dropped at his feet. But unlike Jess, he did not push it away from him.

"Reach," Canavan said a second time.

Again it was Jess who was the first to raise his hands. Walt was a little slow following his companion's lead. But finally he too raised his hands.

"Turn around," Canavan ordered, and he prodded Walt with his gun.

Canavan turned with them so that again he was behind them. But as he bent over to pick up their rifles, Jess, sensing it somehow, whirled around, and lashed out viciously at Canavan's head with his right foot. Unexplainably, unless it was pure instinct that made Canavan anticipate it, he pulled back, reached out with his left hand, and clamped a viselike grip on Jess's foot. He gave it a sudden twist, flipping Jess over and sprawling him out on his face and belly. Moving with surprising swiftness for one of his size, Canavan brushed Walt aside with a sweep of his thick right arm, and as Jess attempted to rise, brought his foot down hard on Jess's head, crushing his face into the ground.

Then Canavan stepped back and said curtly: "All right. Get up."

When Jess did not move, Canavan half-turned to Walt, who was staring at him with wide eyes, and said to him: "Get him up on his feet."

74

Obviously impressed by what he had just witnessed and unwilling to provoke the big redheaded man any further, Walt moved quickly. Crossing in front of Canavan, he bent over Jess and practically hauled him up on his feet. Jess's face was dirt-smudged and bloodied, his eyes glassy. He clung to Walt for a moment or two, then he indicated that he was all right again, brought his hands down, and Walt moved away from him. Jess wiped his mouth with his shirt sleeve, and glared at Canavan.

"You try 'ny more tricks on me, mister, and I won't let you off with a busted nose," Canavan told him. "I'll push it into your face so hard, it'll come out the back of your head. Now turn around like you were before you decided to get smart with me."

But the next time that Canavan bent to pick up the rifles, he was more careful. Bending at the knees but with his body straight, he was able to keep a watchful eye on his captives. Coming erect again with the rifles, he hoisted them, slung them over his left shoulder, and herded Jess and Walt ahead of him into the Emporium through the back door. He halted them when they came to the open cellar door.

"How many o' you buzzards has Had got across the street?" he asked Walt.

"Four more," was the prompt reply. "Counting the sheriff and himself, six."

Jess's battered lips twisted as he said scornfully: "You haven't got a chance. You won't get out of here alive."

Canavan gave him a head-tilted look.

"Mister," he said evenly, "the less I hear outta you, the better I'll like it and the better it'll be for you. You open your mouth to me just once more and I'll put my foot in it. Now move. Get down those stairs, and be quick about it."

Again Walt obeyed without delay. But Jess, who was still glaring at Canavan, did not move. Canavan grabbed him with his free hand, flung him around, and applying the sole of his right boot to Jess's backside, sent him careening down the stairs. Since there was no banister to grab to stop himself, he went hurtling down. Walt, who was almost at the bottom of the stairs, looked up instantly in alarm when he heard Jess's cry, and tried to ward him off. But Jess, with the catapulting effect of Canavan's boot propelling him, came plummeting down upon Walt. There was a muffled cry of pain. The two men tumbled down the rest of the way and wound up on the cellar floor in a tangle of threshing arms and legs. The door above them thumped down and left them in gloomy darkness.

"You lousy bastid!" Jess yelled.

This time Canavan ignored him. Snapping the lock on the

cellar door, he headed for the front of the store to rejoin Tom Bannon.

Bannon was kneeling, hunched over a bit, in the corner that was formed by the window and the open door. He was peering out the window, moving constantly as he twisted his body and craned his neck in order to keep the alleys opposite the Emporium in sight. His difficulty was caused by the farm wagon that Canavan had left drawn up at the curb in front of the store. It blocked off Bannon's view of the street and made it necessary for him to peer through the various spokes of the wagon's wheels to keep track of what was going on across the way. His neck was beginning to resent the demands made of it and his eyes felt tired and strained; the deepening frown that was darkening his face reflected the way he felt. When he heard bootsteps coming from the shadowy rear of the store, his right hand dropped and rested on the butt of his gun, and he twisted around on his haunches. As the footsteps came closer, Bannon half-drew his gun and half-raised up too. When Canavan appeared, he relaxed, shoved the gun down into his holster, and asked: "She make it all right?"

"She made it away from here all right," Canavan answered, unslinging the rifles and laying them on the counter. "Have to wait, though, till Thayer gets back so he can tell us if she made it all right to the bank."

"Uh-huh. You had me a mite worried when you didn't show right back here. Began to wonder if something had happened."

"Two of Had's men, townsmen they looked like to me, were out back. I had to wait till I saw my chance. When it came, I jumped them, took their guns away from them, and locked them up in the cellar."

"Grabbin' off two o' th'm cuts the odds down some. Wonder how many our friend Had's got layin' for us across the street?"

"There are six o' th'm. Had, Peaseley, and four others."

Bannon looked genuinely surprised.

"Mean to say that's all he could round up? If that's the best he could do, he doesn't sound like much of a boss to me. And if those four others aren't any better than Had and old Peaseley, then we haven't anything to worry about."

"We aren't out of here yet, Tom."

"No, we aren't," Bannon agreed. "I don't think they're aiming to rush us, Johnny. Don't think they've got the guts for that. Way it looks to me, they're gonna wait for us to come out so they can gun us down."

"If it wasn't for Elena, if she wasn't around, I'd say they're gonna have a helluva long wait. Now I don't know. Can' just leave her camped on Stonebridge's doorstep, y'know."

There were slow, labored bootsteps outside on the walk, and Bannon, yanking at his holster, swung around with his gun raised. Canavan moved away from the counter and stood motionlessly, facing the door, with his hand curled around the butt of his gun. Ab Peaseley, holding up his bent arms so that Canavan could see that his holster was still empty, appeared in the doorway. Bannon stood up and came out from behind the door.

"Well, well, well," he said, lowering his gun. "If it isn't the law itself. What's your problem, Peaseley?"

"Got something to tell you fellers."

Bannon shot a look at Canavan.

"We're listening," the latter said.

"Don't think you fellers are aware o' this," the sheriff began, lowering his arms, "but we've got you two trapped in here. Got you surrounded, you might say. That is, we've got both doors, the front and the back, covered, and being that they're the only way out of here, it don't look to me like you're gonna get out of here alive." He paused and coughed lightly behind his hand. His spectacles slid down and he frowned, a reflection of his annoyance with them, and pushed them up again on his nose. "Had's willing to let you go," he continued. "But on one condition, and he's willing to take your word that you'll do as you say you will if you take him up on it."

Again Bannon held his tongue and left it to Canavan to answer.

"We're still listening," Canavan said simply.

Peaseley wiped his mouth with the back of his hand.

"This'll prove to you," he said, addressing himself as before to Canavan and ignoring Bannon as though he weren't even there, "that Had isn't as ornery as you think he is. He's willing to live and let live."

"Get to the point, Peaseley," Canavan said curtly.

"Coming right to it. Turn back the O-Bar-O to Stonebridge and let him sell it for you so you c'n get your money out of it, and while he's lookin' around for a buyer, you an' your crew clear out of Indian Head," the sheriff concluded.

"And that's the deal?"

"That's right. You agree to it and I'll go back to Had and tell him you're taking him up on it, and I know that'll be that. Had and the boys will go about their business and you c'n do the same. All right? Is it a deal?"

There were footsteps at the rear, and presently Floyd Thayer, a little out of breath, came hurrying forward to the front of the store. As he neared the counter, he glanced at the two rifles that Canavan had laid across it, raised his eyes, and promptly flushed when he saw Ab Peaseley. He slowed his step and finally stopped altogether.

The sheriff leveled a critical, frowning look at him, and shaking his head, said: "This is all your doing, Floyd. If you hadda done as you were told, none o' this woulda happened. I dunno what to make of you, turning against your kin and sidin' in with strangers. And I don't mind telling you that Had's good an' sore at you. But I'll leave you to him. I'll leave it to him to tell you what he thinks of you."

"Never mind that for now, Peaseley," Canavan said, and the lawman took his eyes from Thayer and turned them again on Canavan. "You can go back to Had and tell him I said it's no deal."

Peaseley looked hard at him for a moment, then his rounded, sloping shoulders lifted a bit.

"If that's the way you want it," he said, "it's all right with me. I didn't expect you to take Had up. Fact is, I woulda been doggoned surprised if you hadda gone along with what he was offering you. I will admit, though, that I was kinda hoping that you would go along with it because that way there wouldn't have to be any gunplay, bloodshed, and killings. But I know you wouldn't go for any peaceful kind o' way of settling things. You've gotta have a chance to use your gun, to show folks how good you are with it. Must be you get some kind o' pleasure outta killing. Well, you'll get your chance now to use your gun. You'll kill some of us. But you won't kill all of us because there'll be too many of us for that. And those of us that are left will kill you. You must know that. But you still want things to wind up that way. Being that we haven't any . . . any alternative, we'll have to go along with things the way you want th'm. I'm sorry for you, mister. Doggoned sorry too. But—"

"Oh, shut up, Peaseley," Bannon said, interrupting him. "You run off at the mouth like an old squaw, and you never shut up. G'wan now. Get outta here. Go tell your boss it's no deal, that we aren't interested in his proposition. And here's something else you might tell him, Flannel-mouth. When we start shooting we'll be looking to get him and you first. Turn yourself around and get going."

"Hold it," someone said behind Floyd Thayer, and all heads including the startled storekeeper's turned and all eyes held on the newcomer. Standing a bare two or three feet beyond Thayer was a blond, smooth-skinned youth who carried his heavily bandaged right wrist in a white muslin sling while he clutched a leveled Colt in his left hand. Canavan recognized him at once. It was Tommy Thayer, who with his two companions, Paulie Voight and the now dead Curly Simmons, had provoked the fight in Ossie Blue's saloon. The muzzle of young Thayer's gun held on a line with the second button on Canavan's shirt "Don't any of you make a move. 'Specially you, *Mister* Canavan. Leastways, not till I say the word. When I do, you redheaded sonuvabitch, go for your gun. I'll have the advantage. But you owe me that. So I'll kill you and Indian Head can go back to being what it was before you horned in on us. Sheriff, you'd better get out of here. And you, Uncle Floyd, get down behind your counter and stay put there till I tell you you can come out. You, mister," the youth said, addressing Bannon. "Unbuckle your gunbelt and when it drops, kick it away."

"No, sonny, I won't," Bannon said evenly. "You've got the drop on us, so you go ahead and shoot. Only remember this. There are two of us and both of us are right handy with our guns. So you c'n depend on it that one of us will get you. That the satisfaction you want, of getting yourself killed?"

Young Thayer moistened his lips with the tip of his tongue.

"I'll tell you again, mister," he said, "only this will be the last time. Unbuckle your gunbelt and——"

"Drop your own gun," a voice that was Elena's said directly behind him and when she straightened up she was holding a leveled shotgun that she poked hard against his spine. "Drop it, I said."

Tommy Thayer flushed. But he needed no further prodding by Elena. His Colt dropped on the floor at his feet.

"Danged fool boy," Floyd Thayer said with a shake of his head. He bent over and picked up the Colt, turned and laid it on the counter, and turning again to his nephew, added severely: "Haven't had enough happen to you, have you? Now you get outta here before your aunt comes hustling down here and takes a strap to you. G'wan now. Get."

The crestfallen Thayer youth, with an angry look at Canavan and a hard stare at Bannon, who stepped back to permit him to pass, hurried out of the store. Suddenly there was a furious pounding of horses' hoofs outside, the beat swelling as the horsemen came on down the street. Bannon, turning and shouldering the sheriff out of his way, went to the doorway and poked his head out. He flung up his hand and yelled something that sounded like a war whoop. Half-turning, grinning broadly, he said: "Kinda think we can finish loading now, boss, and go home. I don't think Mister Had or anybody else will try to stop us. Scotty and the boys musta got tired of waiting for us to show back, so they decided to come and see for themselves what was keeping us."

As Bannon turned again in the doorway, five horsemen came drumming up to the Emporium. Peaseley pushed past Bannon and left the store in a hurry.

NINE

At Canavan's insistence, Elena made a second visit to the bank, to return the shotgun that she had borrowed from Stonebridge. This time, though, she left the Emporium through the front door, hand-shading her eyes as she angled across the deserted, sun-bathed street. Then, as Canavan had instructed her, she was to wait for him in the buggy that stood at the curb in front of the bank.

Canavan and Bannon stood on the walk that fronted Floyd Thayer's general store, and squinted through the parted fingers of their upraised hands in deference to the dazzling sun. While MacNaughton and the others loaded the wagon, the two followed Elena with their narrowed eyes.

When they saw her mount the opposite curb, Bannon remarked: "She's quite a girl."

"You can say that again. When she popped up behind that Thayer kid with that shotgun, I don't mind telling you I breathed a helluva lot easier. The muzzle of that kid's gun kept gaping at me and getting bigger and bigger the longer he pointed it at me, and if he had been able to go through with what he'd set out to do, that would've been it for me. He was so close to me, he couldn't have missed me."

"I know the feeling," Bannon said, and added grimly: "I've had to look into gun muzzles a couple o' times too." But then he said in a lighter tone: "Just as I expected, soon's our friends across the way saw the boys come loopin' down the street, that was it for them."

"Elena just went into the bank."

"I know. I saw her going in. But getting back to Scotty and the others, all anybody needs is one good look at them to know right off that they aren't the kind to shy away from a fight. And that handful o' townsmen who probably couldn't hit the broad side of a barn, 'less they were peggin' lead at it from right smack on top of it, decided they weren't that anxious to die for Had and Indian Head. They sure turned tail and got outta there in a hurry. And when Had saw them quitting on him, he musta realized that if he stayed put there and tried to shoot it out with us, he'd be inviting himself to his own funeral. So he skedaddled too. Proof o' that is the fact that there isn't any sign of them or him that I c'n see."

"Oh, they've gone, all right," Canavan said. "There isn't anybody in any of those alleys across the street." He was silent for a brief moment. Then he continued with: "Y'know, for a while there, it looked to me like the only way we had of breaking out of Thayer's was to shoot our way out."

"Yeah, but with our horses tied up across the street to that pussyfooter's hitch rail, I'm not so sure we could have made it over there all in one piece. Then, even though the wagon's right out here, no more'n a hop, skip, an' a jump from the door, it was right under the eyes and the rifles of Had's bunch, so I'm not so sure we could have made it to that either. Wouldn't have taken any extra slick shooting to've cut us down. And if we had made it out to the wagon, we still wouldn't have got very far with it. Those buzzards over there," and he nodded at the opposite side of the street, "could've turned their rifles loose on the team, and we'd have found ourselves pinned down in an open wagon right out in the middle of the street. And that woulda been a helluva lot worse for us than it was inside Thayer's."

"That's right," Canavan agreed.

"But the picture's changed, and I'm not sorry. Soon's the boys finish loading up the wagon, we'll head for home, and that'll be that. I'll bet that Had, wherever he is now, must be fit t'be tied thinking that he had us right where he wanted us only to lose us. And who knows if he'll ever be able to ketch us that way again?"

There was constant movement of men and supplies from the store to the wagon, then a retracing of bootsteps to bring out more to stow away in the wagon that was rapidly filling up.

"Y'know, losing us when he thought he had us could be awf'lly discouraging to Had. Think it might lead him to lay off?"

"Nope. Not Had. When a man like him sets his mind to something, he keeps plugging away at it till he succeeds or gets himself killed."

The movement of men to and from the store came to an end, a sign that the last of the Canavan purchases had been removed from the Emporium. Tall, lean, dark-complexioned MacNaughton came sauntering out hitching up his levis. He halted at Bannon's side, and said: "That's it, Tom."

Half-turning, Bannon repeated it to Canavan. "That's it, Johnny."

"Good. Then we can get rolling. The sooner we shake the dust of this place off our boots, the better I'll like it."

"Have one of the boys do the driving," Bannon instructed MacNaughton. "You others kinda flank the wagon. Boss and me'll take the lead."

"Right," Scotty said. He stepped down into the gutter and joined the other four men who were standing about idly between their horses and the wagon.

When one of the men led his horse around the wagon to the tailgate and tied him to it, rounded the wagon to the front of it, and climbed up to the driver's seat, Bannon said to Canavan: "Think you oughta know the names of the men you've got riding for you, Johnny. And which one's which. That's Lee Dwyer doing the driving. The one Scotty's talking to now, that kinda heavy-set feller, is Dutch Haber. The two on their horses are Phil Sawyer and Andy Jeffords. Phil's the sandy-haired one."

Canavan's gaze had focused on each man as Bannon identified him. He shot a quick look up the street. When he saw Elena followed by Stonebridge emerge from the bank and cross the walk to the waiting buggy, he said: "There's Elena now. Let's go."

Together Bannon and Canavan marched across the street to the rail in front of the sheriff's office, untied their horses, and climbed up on them. Bannon wheeled his mount away from the rail. He reined in and looked back wonderingly when Canavan, instead of following him, sat motionlessly astride the hoof-pawing mare, and stared at the window in Peaseley's office. Bannon knee-nudged his horse back to Canavan's side.

"S'matter?" he asked.

Canavan didn't answer. Instead he backed the mare away from the rail. Bannon wheeled away from it a second time, and as Canavan came up alongside him, and the two started up the street, Canavan said: "Had was standing at the window, staring out, but without seeing anything. Leastways that's the way it seemed to me. Suddenly, though, he raised his eyes, and when he saw me, he gave me the damnedest look. If looks c'n kill, guess I should be dead now."

"The hell with him," Bannon said bluntly.

When they came abreast of the waiting horsemen and the heavily loaded wagon, Bannon gestured, and rode on with

Canavan. The mounted men backed to the curb to permit the wagon to turn. When it made its turn and had straightened out and was actually underway, its broad, iron-rimmed wheels crunching and grinding the gutter dirt, MacNaughton and the others moved after it and took up flanking positions around it.

Stonebridge was standing at the curb talking with Elena, who had seated herself in the buggy and, reins in hand, was waiting for Canavan. As he came alongside, she turned her head, lifted her eyes to him, and smiled.

"You might as well go on, Tom," Canavan said to Bannon, who had reined in at his side. "We'll catch up with you."

"Sure," Bannon said, and trotted off.

The wagon and its escort of outriders came rumbling up. Elena's eyes widened when she saw the pile-up of things in the wagon.

"Goodness, John, did we buy all those things?" she asked.

He grinned at her.

"Yep," he answered, and twisting around in the saddle, ranged his gaze after the wagon as it toiled on behind Bannon. He squared around again and said to Stonebridge: "Thanks again. That shotgun of yours got me out of a tight spot."

"No credit due me, Canavan. All I did was supply the shotgun. Your wife did the rest. So your thanks should go to her."

"It did. Chances are I wouldn't be here now if it hadn't been for her." He reached down and squeezed her arm.

"Have you bought any stock yet?" Stonebridge asked him.

"Haven't had either the time or a chance to do that."

"Perhaps I can be of some service to you in that direction. Ed Stoner is quitting, selling out, and going back east to Philadelphia to live with his widowed daughter. Ed runs a herd of some fifteen hundred head. He doesn't want to sell off small bunches. He wants to make a deal for the whole herd, and in an effort to attract a buyer, he's willing to shade the price. He'll take half cash, the balance in notes, if he has to. Although he'd much prefer to be paid off in full at one time. And if it's a cash sale, he might be induced to shade the price even more. You interested?"

"I sure am. This Stoner, he from around here?"

Stonebridge shook his head. "No. From around Humboldt way. That's the county seat."

"I know. You get me a price from him, will you? For cash, that is. If the price is reasonable, he'll have a deal for himself."

"Fine," the banker said, nodding. "Oh, here's something else for you to think about. Stoner's let most of his crew go.

All except his three top hands. They aren't kids. They're good, matured, experienced hands whom he's known for a long time and whom he heartily recommends. Think you might want to add them to your crew?"

"Could be. While I'm thinking about them, if you'll find out what he wants for his stock—?"

"I expect to see him either late today or early tomorrow morning. Suppose I bring him out to your place? That be all right?"

" 'Course."

Suddenly Canavan stiffened and slowly sat upright in the saddle. His eyes hardened and his lips tightened. Slowly too his right hand moved downward to the butt of his gun and curled around it.

Stonebridge looked wonderingly at him, turned his head, and followed Canavan's steely gaze with his own eyes. Standing a few feet back from the entrance to one of the alleys that flanked the bank building was a slim youth who carried his right wrist in a sling and who seemed to be holding something in his left hand that he was trying to conceal behind the sling. It was, of course, Tommy Thayer.

"Apparently that young man doesn't know when to stop," Stonebridge said quietly, "or that his luck may well run out on him if he persists and presses it too far."

Elena glanced at the banker, a puzzled look on her face.

"What's he doing? Trying to hide something behind his sling?" the banker asked. "I can't tell for sure from here."

"It's a gun," Canavan answered, without taking his eyes off the Thayer boy, "and he doesn't want me to see it till he's ready to use it."

"Oh!" Stonebridge said.

There was no need for either of the two men to tell her that it was Tommy Thayer whom they were talking about. She sensed it, and twisted around, and when she spottted the persistent youth she paled.

"What are you doing there, boy?" the banker called to him. "What do you want?"

There was no reply.

"Think you'd better pull up a ways," Canavan said to Elena. "I don't want you caught in that fool kid's line of fire if he decides to shoot."

"If I'm in his way, he won't shoot," she protested.

"Don't count on that. I think he's crazy enough to shoot no matter who's between him and me. Go on, honey. Do's I say, please. Pull up a little ways. And I think you'd better move with her, Stonebridge."

"Harebrained young fool," the latter muttered darkly.

But he moved when Elena and the buggy did, kept pace with it, and when she halted it some fifteen or twenty feet away, he stopped too.

"All right, Thayer," Canavan called to him. He swung down from the mare, slapped her on the rump with his left hand, and ignored her nasally pitched protest when she trotted away. "Nobody in the way now. So make your play. I'm ready for you. Only before you go off half-cocked, think this over. If I have to shoot, I won't wing you as I did last time. I'll put a bullet right smack into the middle of you. Now it's up to you whether you live or die."

Young Thayer was motionless for a moment or two. Then as Canavan watched him, he began to retreat down the slightly sloping length of the alley that was half in shadows, half in thin sunlight. He passed the midway point, slowly backtracking, one foot at a time, moving so unhurriedly and so deliberately that it made Canavan think to himself: "Forcing himself to back down slowly so that he won't give in to panic and run."

Then the youth was past the three-quarter mark, and Canavan could see bright sunshine at the end of the alley begin to silhouette him. Finally Tommy was within a single step of the bank's back yard. As he took a last backward step that would bring him into the yard, he yanked his gun out and flung a shot at Canavan, wheeled around and fled. Canavan made no attempt to draw and shoot.

The wildly fired bullet that missed him failed to bring any of the townspeople out to the street to see what was going on. But it brought Ossie Blue out from behind the bar and out to the walk in front of his place.

Glancing up the street, Canavan saw Elena and Stonebridge looking at him, Elena standing upright in the buggy with her clenched right fist pressed against her lips.

"Be right with you," he called to her. He turned and started downstreet, his boot-toes kicking up tiny clouds of dust from the parched gutter dirt.

After a couple of strides, he stepped up on the walk and marched on. As he came abreast of Blue's saloon, the aproned proprietor sauntered out to the curb, his long apron flapping around his ankles.

"That shot a minute ago," Ossie said. "Somebody peg it at you?"

"Yeah. That Thayer kid."

"Huh? The Thayer kid?" Ossie repeated. "He must be crazy. He in such a sweat to get himself killed?"

"Whether he is or not, he'll get it good from me if he potshots me again."

The mare came loping down the street, whinnying, with her empty stirrups swinging a little wildly and thumping against her sides. When she had overtaken Canavan, she slowed herself and trotted along with him. When he came to the sheriff's office, he stopped, motioned to her to wait, and added: "All right now. Stay put here."

Obediently she nosed into the hitch rail and he slanted across the walk and went inside. Ab Peaseley, with his battered hat riding on the back of his uncombed head, was standing behind his desk. Had Voight, seeing Canavan enter, turned his back on him, stepped away from the desk where he had been talking with the sheriff, sauntered across the office to the far side wall, and stood facing it.

Peaseley and his spectacles put on their usual performance; the spectacles slid down his nose almost to the very tip of it and he promptly pushed them up again, a little more roughly this time than usual. With his hands on his hips and his head tilted a bit to one side, he eyed Canavan and said: "I heard that shot and I was just gonna go out to see who you'd gunned down this time."

Canavan frowned. He resisted an almost overpowering urge to reach across the desk, tear the tarnished star off the sheriff's shirt, and cram it down his throat.

"That Thayer kid took a shot at me from an alley," he said evenly.

"Being that I only heard one shot, that means you let him get away with it," Peaseley said, and his arched shaggy eyebrows reflected his surprise. "How come you didn't go after him and fix him like you did that other kid, that Curly Simmons?"

Ignoring the sheriff's question, Canavan said: "You're always sounding off about you being the law here. Now act like a lawman. Go find that kid and tell him to quit plaguing me. Because if he doesn't—"

"You'll kill him like you did young Simmons."

Tight-lipped and angry-eyed, Canavan looked hard at him, and finally said: "Forget it, Peaseley. Instead you think about this. I've just about had a bellyful of you and your boss. If you two wanna stay alive, shake the dust of Indian Head while there's still time. Because I've just decided that soon's I get things organized out at my place, I'm taking over the town and I don't want either o' you two around to stink it up on me."

Peaseley was crimson-faced, the flush ranging downward to his neck and throat and upward to his temples. He gulped and swallowed hard, winced and swallowed a second time,

87

and finally sputtered: "Now you hold it right there, mister, and—"

He didn't finish. Canavan lunged across the desk and even though the sheriff reacted instinctively, sought to pull back out of his reach, there was no denying Canavan. He ripped the star off Peaseley's shirt, taking with it a handful of cloth, leaving a jagged tear in the shirt that revealed a span of greyish-looking undershirt. Peaseley, with his mouth open and his normally heavy-lidded eyes bulging, stared at him. Apparently he had been so thoroughly shocked, he couldn't do anything but stare.

"You're finished, Peaseley," Canavan told him, and the man's mouth slowly closed. His eyeballs retracted, and his eyes resumed their half-open look. "You aren't the law around here any longer. Fact is you aren't anything. Indian Head'll get itself a new sheriff and he won't be anything like you, a-scared of your own shadow, a pussyfooter and a flannel-mouth. He'll be his own man and he'll stand on his own two feet."

He walked to the door, half-opened it, and looked back. Peaseley was ashen-faced. Had Voight had turned and now he stood facing Canavan, stiffly erect with his eyes blazing and the muscles in his lean jaws twitching. "If you know what's good for you, Voight," Canavan said to him, "you'll take the advice you offered me. You'll sell out and clear out of Indian Head. If you don't, you'll be sorry. This town isn't big enough for the two of us, and being that I'm here to stay, and run it, there won't be any room here for you."

Turning again, Canavan opened the door. A gun roared with the authoritative voice of a Colt, and Canavan flung himself backward as a bullet, obviously fired from something of an angle, struck and buried itself in the wall beyond him, gouging out some plaster and cracking the wall for several inches in every direction from the bullet hole. Crouching with his gun in his hand, Canavan suddenly bolted out, flinging a shot above a moving figure that he had already spied in an alley diagonally opposite Peaseley's office. As he dashed across the street, pegging still another shot in the general direction of young Thayer, the latter darted down the alley, skidded to a stop at the foot of it, wheeled and fired again at Canavan, and without waiting to see the result of his second shot, scurried away out of sight.

Canavan did not pursue the youth. He panted to a stop in the entrance to the alley, reloaded his gun, and shoved it down in his holster.

"That kid and his potshots are getting under my skin," he muttered darkly to himself as he turned and headed upstreet.

88

"He's gonna force me to do something I don't wanna do. So for his sake, I hope he smartens up and quits this. If he doesn't, I won't have 'ny alternative."

He glanced across the street. Ab Peaseley and a darkly scowling Had Voight were framed in the open doorway of the former's office, their gaze holding on him. When Had's eyes and Canavan's met, Had muttered something to the sheriff.

"Bet I rocked those two right down to the soles of their flat feet," Canavan murmured. Then to himself he thought: "And from the looks they're giving me, I know damned well what they're hoping. That that pesky kid puts a slug in me. Only thing that can save their hides. They know it and so do I. I hope to hell he disappoints them."

He tramped on, alertly watchful as he neared an alley, slowing his step each time and half-drawing his gun in case his tormentor should suddenly appear. But nothing happened. There was no further sign of the Thayer youth. Nevertheless, Canavan refused to accept that as a good omen, an indication that Tommy had decided to abandon his hounding of him. He was simply laying low, biding his time for a more favorable opportunity, Canavan insisted. So he refused to relax his watchfulness, and went on as alertly as before.

He was about midway between two alleys when the mare came loping up alongside of him with a flurry of hoofbeats, moved in closer to the curb, and whinnied. She was a little taken back, and showed it in the way she halted abruptly in her tracks and looked at him obliquely when he gestured, waving her off. She did not understand. Wisely she obeyed without protest or question, permitting him to keep ahead of her while she followed him at a discreet though somewhat uncertain distance, holding herself down to a mere jog but ready upon signal to quicken her pace and come drumming up to him. A couple of townsmen, defying the sun's wilting rays and braving the stifling heat that still lay so heavily over Indian Head, came plodding along and lifted curious eyes to him. He pretended not to notice and marched on a little more briskly. As he neared the Emporium, he cut across the street. The heavily loaded farm wagon had left the gutter wheel-rutted, he noticed. The mare, refusing to be left behind, continued her dogged following of him, and crossed the street too, but she carefully maintained her measured jogging and the distance between them. As he stepped up on the curb and strode on upstreet, he saw that Elena had climbed down from the buggy and was standing on the walk at Stonebridge's side, and that both of them were looking at him. She said something to the banker, and Canavan saw him nod. Then Elena came hurrying to meet Canavan. They came together shortly.

"Sorry," he told her. "Didn't mean to keep you waiting so long in the hot sun."

As though she hadn't heard him, she said: "John, I'm beginning to doubt the wisdom of our staying on here." To himself he thought: "Uh-huh, here it comes. She's scared and wants to get away from here." She went on with: "We're unwelcome strangers here. And when you come to where a boy holds your life in his hands, that's too much. I've been discussing things with Mr. Stonebridge. He's a very understanding man, John, totally unlike most of the other bankers with whom I've had dealings. Since he would feel responsible, indirectly of course, if anything were to happen to you, he's willing to cancel the deal for the ranch and refund our money. What do you think?"

"Judging by what you've just said, you wanna pull outta here, right?"

She hesitated for a moment before she answered, and when she did, she said emotionally: "I don't really know what I want. Normally, I don't scare easily. So on one hand, I want to stay and fight. But on the other hand, frankly because I'm frightened, I want to get away from here as quickly as possible."

"Uh-huh. So you're putting it up to me to decide for the two of us."

"Yes," she said simply. But then she added: "I know it isn't fair to you."

"I wanna do everything that I think will make you happy."

"I know that, John. And I love you for it."

He rubbed his chin reflectively with the back of his hand and said: "I need a shave. Guess my hair needs cutting too." He cupped his chin in his hand and smiled down into her earnest face:"So what do I say?" Suddenly remembering, he dug in his pants pocket, fished out Peaseley's star, and held it up for her to see. She looked at it and lifted puzzled eyes to him. "No," he said. "It's not for me. I quit being a lawman a long time ago and I haven't any hankering to be one again. I'm a cattleman now and I aim to go on being one for a long, long time to come. I had it out with Peaseley when I went to ask him if he wouldn't get hold of that Thayer kid and talk some sense into him. Instead, that old washwoman sassed me, and when I'd heard enough out of him, I told him he was through, that Indian Head didn't want any more of him, and that we'd come up with somebody else to do his job. Somebody who wasn't an old flannel-mouthed pussyfooter like him. Then I tore the star off his shirt."

"Goodness," she said. "You really were angry, weren't you?"

"Yeah, guess I was. Had was there. But he wouldn't even look at me. Stood with his back to me and his face to the wall. I told Peaseley that everything I'd said to him was meant for his boss too, and wound up by telling th'm that I was gonna take over Indian Head and run it. When I started to leave, Had turned around. Oh-h, he was fighting mad. I let him have it right to his face. Told him that Indian Head isn't big enough for the two of us, and being that I'm here to stay, the best thing he c'n do for himself is clear out, or he'll be sorry."

"Then you don't want to go. You want to stay."

"Like I said before, Elena, I want to do what you want me to do. What'll make you happy. If you wanna pull up stakes and go somewhere's else, that's what we'll do."

She shook her head and said quietly: "No, John. Have you forgotten what I told you before we married, that whatever decisions had to be made, you would make them? That still goes. So we'll stay here, and whoever doesn't like having us here—"

He grinned a little and said: "C'n go fly a kite, right?"

"Right. Now what about that Thayer boy? Can't something be done about him?"

"Like what?"

"Isn't there someone we can go to, someone who has some influence with him who can get him to stop this . . . this mad thing he's set out to do?"

" 'Fraid not, honey."

"Then what are you supposed to do? Let him go on shooting at you till he finally kills you?"

"You must know the answer to that same's I do."

"You mean the only way you can stop him from going on with this is by killing him."

"I don't want to, believe me. But he isn't leaving me any alternative, is he?"

"Let's go home, John. I think I've had enough of Indian Head for today."

"I'm ready to go when you are."

"I'm ready now."

Hand-in-hand, they went up the street to where Stonebridge and the buggy were waiting. When Canavan whistled, the mare responded with a happy whinny and came trotting up to him, nuzzled him, and was delighted when he patted her. Minutes later, having taken their leave of Stonebridge, they headed for home.

91

TEN

The ribbony span of open, sun-bathed roadway that led eastward from Indian Head was deserted. It ran between two farflung stretches of fenced-in grassy tableland that upgraded from the shoulders of the road and leveled off about three feet above it, where the fences began. Casting an appraising glance at one side and then at the other, Canavan wondered why there was no sign of cattle since the land appeared to be ideal for grazing purposes. Perhaps the heat and the wilting sun were responsible for their removal farther inland, he conceded, where water was close by. Then a hundred feet or so ahead, he spotted a lone horse nibbling on some grass close to a fence post. The horse looked up almost instantly when he heard the approaching rumble of wheels and hoofbeats, whinnied a couple of times, and poked his head through the lower and upper strands of wire. He eyed the oncoming horses with interest. When they came abreast of him, he hastily withdrew his head and loped along the fence, keeping pace with them and prancing gaily every now and then in an effort to attract their attention. But after a while, when the heat began to exact its toll of him and he became discouraged by the other horses' lack of interest in him, he pulled up abruptly and snorted half in anger and half in scorn. Then he wheeled around and jogged back to the fence post that he had so willingly abandoned for them.

When they came to where the road was tree-lined and tree-shaded, Elena said with a lift of her eyes to Canavan and a wan smile: "This is better, isn't it?"

"And how it is," Canavan replied.

Twice the mare whinnied softly and looked around at Canavan and each time Elena saw him twist around in the saddle and look back. But he said nothing when he squared around, and the only inkling she had of impending trouble was a frown that had already begun to deepen on his face.

"What is it, John?"

"She," he said and Elena knew that he meant the mare. "She can hear something a mile off. I can't see anything and I can't hear anything either. But when she makes a to-do like she's done twice already, I'm willing to take her word for it that somebody's coming."

"You mean following us, don't you?"

He didn't answer.

"That Thayer boy?" she pressed him.

"Doesn't have to be him, y'know. Could be somebody else. Somebody heading for one o' the spreads . . . one o' the ranches. There are a lot o' th'm around here."

She made no response. Her silence and the expression on her face reflected his failure to reassure her.

They went on. Suddenly the mare whinnied again, and this time Canavan swung her around.

"Gonna have a look," he announced. "We aren't hittin' it up any. So if there's somebody coming, he shoulda caught up with us by now and maybe even passed us. 'Less, of course, he's purposely hanging back."

She could have told him that that was what she was thinking too. But she held her tongue.

"Be right back," he told her over his shoulder as he loped off.

The mare's hoofbeats shattered the silence that lay all about the area. Elena sat half-turned in the buggy, her anxious eyes holding on the rapidly disappearing Canavan. The drumming beat of the mare's hoofs faded out, and Canavan disappeared into the distance. She sat motionlessly, in fact rigidly, biting her lower lip. The minutes passed long drawn-out minutes. But nothing happened to shatter the pall-like silence. More minutes went by, and they were just as uneventful as the others. But then so suddenly, startling her and making her catch her breath, it did happen. There was a sudden burst of gunfire. She couldn't tell for certain if there were two or three shots fired. But she reacted instantly. She squared around, startling the buggy horse when she jerked the lines and whacked him on the rump with the loose ends, and sent him pounding away after Canavan. She hadn't gone very far, probably no more than half a mile, when she heard oncoming hoofbeats. Raising up a bit and peering anxiously into the hazy sunlight of the open road ahead of her, she finally spied a horseman coming toward her at a swift canter. She recognized him almost immediately after, and breathed a deep sigh of relief as Canavan came steadily closer. She halted the buggy and sat back and waited for him to come up to her. Her horse stood head-bowed and spread-legged and proceeded to blow himself.

Canavan had already spotted her too. He slowed the mare to a trot and then to a mere jog. He pulled up alongside of the buggy, slacked a little in the saddle, and told Elena: "It was that young squirt again. Didn't see him right off. When he heard me coming he managed to get that horse of his, an old plug he was too, up that upgrade to the fence. He found a spot that had a break in it, and there he sat, waiting inside the fence, for me to come closer. I didn't look up there. Instead I was looking for him somewhere's along the road, maybe layin' for me in one of the . . . the shoulders. You know, where the ground kinda dips and drops away from the road itself. The first I knew where he was was when he pegged two shots at me. Took me by surprise all right. Before I could do anything about it, he was through the break and hightailing it. I tried to go after him. But she—" and he reached down and patted the mare—"but she couldn't make it. Slipped and slid down both times. I quit then. Didn't want to take a chance on her hurting herself."

"I think it's quite obvious, John, that that boy intends to keep on with this . . . this bedeviling of you," Elena said.

"Sure looks that way. Only here's why you don't have to go worrying yourself sick over me. He's had five, six shots at me and he's missed me every time. And missed me by a lot too. So if that's the best he can do, if he had 'ny sense he'd quit."

"Don't look for him to do that."

"I don't. But I'll tell you what I've already made up my mind to do if he takes just one more shot at me. I'll forget he's only a sprout, and I'll go after him no matter where I have to follow him to catch up with him. And when I do catch up with him, that'll be it for him. All I hope is that the next time he's where I see him right off."

Elena wheeled the buggy, and Canavan backed the mare in order to give her room to make the turn. As she completed it and straightened out, he rode after her, came up alongside of the buggy, and rode on with it.

They were within a mile or so of the newly named "JC" when the keen-eared mare suddenly whinnied a warning that someone was coming. Instantly Elena looked up at Canavan, concern in her eyes and manner.

"Think it's that awful Thayer boy again?" she asked.

Canavan shook his head.

"Don't see how he coulda circled around and got that far ahead of us. Must be somebody else," he replied.

Elena raised up and peered hard into the shadowy road that ran ruler-straight for another couple of hundred feet and then quite suddenly and abruptly veered off and took a sharp curve that was shut off from view by a wall of wild brush and screening trees. Slowing their horses, they rode on as before, guardedly though, with their eyes fixed upon the straightaway's end. Canavan had his hand on his gun as he waited for the oncoming horseman to emerge from the bend and appear in the open. Now they could hear the rhythmic beat of a horse's hoofs. The beat swelled, and then very suddenly, startling the tensed-up Elena, a mounted man came loping around the curve and practically burst into the open and drummed on toward them, instinctively slowing his horse the moment he spotted them. He was a big man, burly too, and he carried his right arm in a sling just as Tommy Thayer did, and handled the reins with his left hand. As he came steadily closer, Canavan, eyeing him, relaxed and took his hand off his gun butt.

Elena, who had just shot a look at him, relaxed too, but not quite as completely as Canavan had, and asked: "He someone you know, John?"

"Uh-huh," he told her. "Al Voight. Had's brother."

An expression of alarm came into her face.

"You going to tell him what happened, and what you told Had?" she wanted to know.

"Sure. Al isn't a bad sort. He knows that Had's been in the wrong with me all along. But because they're brothers, he can't admit it. Leastways not right out, or in so many words."

Elena and the two men reined in when they came together in the middle of the road.

'Well, what d'you know! Mister Al Voight himself," Canavan said childishly. "On account o' you I got up extra early and wore myself out waiting for you to show up at my place with Had's stock. And don't tell me you forgot, because I know better. Old Man Peaseley came over instead o' you and he spilled the beans. Told me you were at Had's place. What's that for?" And he pointed to the sling. "What's the matter with your arm? You really hurt it, or is the sling just an excuse you came up with to save you from getting a nice lead slug I had ready for you?"

The burly Voight flushed. "Lemme know when you're finished," he retorted.

"On the level now, wasn't it a case o' cold feet that kept you away?"

"Figured you'd think that."

"How else was I supposed to figure it?"

Shifting himself a little in the saddle, Al said: " 'Course you won't believe me when I tell you, not that it matters any to me. But if you think you can listen for, say, one whole minute without horning in on me, I'll tell you what happened."

"I'm all ears," Canavan said with a grin.

"Like I said I would, I was all set to drive Had's herd across your place to that stream. Only a couple o' things that Had shouldn'ta said but did anyway got me sore and I started to walk out on him. I dunno what I tripped over. Could be it was my own feet. Anyway over I went. Like a poled steer. Landed right smack on my arm. Hurt like all get-out. So I went back to my place and sent one o' my hands hustling to town to fetch Doc Anderson. The doc came back with him, took a look at my arm, and told me I'd busted it. He did what he had to do, and that was that. That's the story, Mac, of how you didn't scare me any and why I didn't show up at your place to prove it."

"Sounds reasonable," Canavan commented. "So I'm willing to go along with it."

Voight grinned a little. "Thanks," he answered. "Thanks a lot. That oughta make the arm feel better."

"I should think you'd be a lot better off at home," Elena said. "All that jouncing around you must be getting must make the arm hurt all the more."

Al had only glanced at Elena before, confining his eyes and his remarks to Canavan. Now he turned his head and leveled a full look at her. He finally took off his hat, a little clumsily because he was holding the reins in his only workable hand, and said: "I wouldn't expect him," and he jerked his head at Canavan, "to know what's right and proper like introducing us, ma'am. In case you didn't catch it, the name's Voight. Al Voight."

"I did catch it, Mr. Voight. I'm Elena Canavan."

He bowed his head the barest bit. "Pleasure to know you ma'am. Sorry I can't say that about your brother . . ."

"And I'm sorry I can't say something nice about your brother."

"Oh-h, Had isn't the worst kind. Just happens that your brother and he started off on the wrong foot. That's all."

"I think I'd better tell you this before you go saying anything more about my brother. I wish I had one. Unfortunately, I haven't. I'm Mrs. Canavan."

Voight pretended to be so thoroughly shocked by her disclosure that he was rendered speechless for the moment. Open-mouthed, he stared wide-eyed at her.

Elena giggled. "Oh, come now, Mr. Voight!"

96

"You mean you're that . . . that big redheaded galoot's wife?"

"That's right."

"I'll be doggoned! How'd he get you to marry him? Probably sweet-talked you into it, huh? Or did he hold a gun to your head?"

"No, he didn't do either of those things. He didn't have to. I married him quite willingly. Very happily too, I might add."

Al was unconvinced. "I think you shoulda waited a while longer. I'm sure you woulda done better for yourself. Somebody else would probably have come along. Might even have been me. And look how much better off you woulda been."

"Look, you overstuffed buffalo, you want me to break the other arm for you?" Canavan demanded of him. Then: "I tangled with Had again today, Al."

Reluctantly the bulky Voight took his plainly appreciative eyes off Elena and turned his gaze on Canavan.

"What was it about this time?"

Simply and without embellishment of any kind, Canavan related the events that had led to his final ultimatum to Had and Peaseley. Al listened quietly to Canavan's recital, and when it was finished, he sat motionlessly astride his horse, troubled looking and silent and offering nothing. Elena's gaze shuttled between the two men. Canavan waited. But when Al failed to say anything, Canavan's impatience overcame him, and he demanded: "Well? Haven't you got anything to say?"

"Yeah, sure. I've got something to say. Only you won't like it when you hear it."

"Say it anyway."

"All right. I kinda think you've bitten off a heckuva bigger piece than you can chew."

"Go on," Canavan commanded.

" 'Course there isn't any way for you to know this, Canavan, being that you're a stranger here. But there are a lot o' people around these parts who think Had's good for them and for Indian Head too. So when the chips are down, you'll find them line up behind Had and ready to back his play. So driving him outta Indian Head isn't gonna be the lead-pipe cinch you mighta thought it'd be. I don't think you want any advice outta me. After all, I'm a Voight, and Had's my brother, and blood's still thicker'n water. But because that pretty little lady of yours stands to lose a lot if you try to take on the whole town and wind up with a slug in your gut, I'm gonna give you some advice anyway. Think things out real good, Canavan, before you make your move to chase Had out of Indian Head."

There was no comment, no response from Canavan. Voight, who had paused deliberately in order to give Canavan an opportunity to answer him, finally continued with: "Far as Ab Peaseley's concerned, he doesn't mean a thing to me, and far as I know, not to anyone else either 'cept maybe to Had. But I wouldn't wanna bet on that. Even though Had's my brother, I've gotta admit that Had's for Had, first, last, and always, and if Ab hasn't served the purpose that Had hired him for, and it comes to a showdown, Ab'll have to face it alone. I don't think Had'll lift a finger to save him. So that brings us down to the Thayer boy, Tommy."

"I'm gonna have t'do something about him," Canavan said.

"It's all right with me," Al said. "His ma and pa are my cousins, and they're good people. But that kid o' theirs is a bad one. 'Less I miss my guess, he'll wind up at the end of a rope. 'Less of course," he added quickly, "you beat the hangman to it. Couple o' years ago, when Tommy was about fourteen or fifteen, he sassed me good about something. While I don't remember what it was, I haven't forgotten the lip that snotty-nosed kid gave me. I whacked him good for it. He's shied away from me ever since. All the same, every time I see him I get the feling that that young squirt's just bidin' his time, that one day when I'm not expecting it or I'm not lookin' too sharp, he'll pay me back for the whackin' I gave him. It'll be a bullet in my back from an alley when nobody's around to see who did it, or a knifeblade in my ribs when it's dark out." He smiled a little wryly and shook his head and said: "We-ll you wanted to know if I didn't have anything to say, didn't you? Seems to me I've said more the last couple o' minutes than I usu'lly do in a couple of hours."

When he looked at Elena, she smiled.

"Been real nice meeting you, ma'am," he told her. "Maybe things'll work themselves out in spite of what's happened so far and we can be friends. Kinda think I'd like that. 'Bye."

He clapped his hat on his head, as clumsily as he had taken it off earlier, and yanked down the brim. Canavan backed the mare a couple of steps, almost crowding her into the buggy, to give Al passing room. The latter grunted, gave Canavan a nod, knee-nudged his horse into movement, and trotted away.

For a minute or so after Al had gone, Canavan and Elena sat silently thoughtful, and motionless too.

"Well, Elena?" Canavan asked. "What do you think? Think I'm letting us in for even more trouble than we've got already?"

"You were faced with practically the same kind of situation

in Truxton, weren't you?" she countered. "With Nick Arvey and all the others opposing you? And even I opposed you. That is, in the beginning. But that didn't stop you, did it? You took them on and beat them. What Al Voight said may well be true. Yet I wonder if he didn't overestimate his brother Had's strength and following among the townspeople of Indian Head."

"Could be. Only one way to find out, huh?"

"Only one way," she repeated.

"I'll have to go through with what I told Had and Peaseley."

"I don't see that you have any alternative, John. Unless we accept Mr. Stonebridge's offer and go somewhere else."

"Every town I've ever been in there's always been somebody who didn't like strangers. Somebody with big ideas who didn't want anybody who mightn't knuckle down to him and maybe spoil whatever he might have going for him. So if we quit Indian Head and go somewhere's else, how d'we know we won't run right smack into the same kind o' setup we've got here? How d'we know there won't be another Had Voight there for us to deal with, or maybe another Nick Arvey, and what'll we do then? Move on again? If we do, pickin' up and heading for some other place will get to be a habit with us, and all of a sudden one day we'll find that there aren't any more places left for us to move on to, that we've made the circuit and that we've finally run out of places that we haven't tried."

"I know that, John. Eventually that's bound to happen to us. So to avoid its happening to us, we might as well save ourselves wear and tear, stay here as we decided to do a while ago, and fight back. We've got to take root somewhere, John, so despite its shortcomings, I suppose Indian Head's about as good a place for that as any."

"Maybe even a lot better than most other places."

"Yes. Let's go home, John."

"Sure," he answered. He squared back in the saddle, but just as they were about to ride on, something that he suddenly remembered stayed him. Elena pulled up abruptly and lifted questioning eyes to him. "Just came to me that you never did get to eat that breakfast you were so starved for."

"No, I didn't. Too many things happened and I forgot I was hungry. But I'm not that hungry now. So I can wait till we get home. Then Maria can fix us something."

"She'll have a lot more to do than just fix something for us. Got six more mouths to feed, and I don't ever remember seeing or hearing about any cowhands who couldn't do a top job with a knife an' fork."

This time Elena held back and waited for Canavan to move out first. When the sleek mare pranced off with him, Elena followed them, quickened the pace of the buggy horse, and came up alongside Canavan before he realized that he had gotten ahead of her. They wheeled into the bend in the road, the horses' hoofs drumming and lifting an echoing metallic clatter that carried far beyond them. They completed the curve and emerged onto another straightaway.

Although her thoughts were not as free from worry as she had pretended just minutes before, she was determined not to let Canavan know how she really felt about staying on in Indian Head. He would have enough to contend with, she maintained to herself, without saddling him with her fears, for she knew that if she admitted them to him, they would prove more disturbing to him than all the Had Voights put together. He would blame himself for staying where they weren't wanted, and even though the thought of letting anyone force him into pulling up stakes and going somewhere else would go against his grain, she knew that he would do it for her sake.

She stole a quick look at him. The set of his jaw, the ominous glint in his steady eyes, the graceful ease with which he rode with the reins in his left hand and his big, strong right hand resting on his thigh with the jutting butt of his gun within instant reach . . . just looking at him gave her strength. There was little need for her to be so concerned, she told herself. Just as Nick Arvey and the rest of the lawless element who had taken over Truxton had found out, he was not the ordinary kind of man. He was not the kind who panicked in the face of overwhelming odds. Quick to size up any situation, when he moved it was with such sudden and deadly swiftness, he usually took his opponent or opponents completely by surprise. This, together with the pulverizing force with which he struck, generally proved to be a devastating combination. So if the Voights, and Al who had made it quite clear that he would have to side in with his brother with his "blood's thicker'n water, y'know" remark, and the whole of Indian Head banded together in an effort to crush Canavan by sheer weight of numbers, they would learn to their sorrow that it couldn't be done. Every assignment that he had ever undertaken in his long years of service with the Rangers found him pitted against a town, corrupt officials or politicians, or as in the case of Truxton, against a band of lawless men who rode roughshod over anyone who dared oppose them. That he had emerged safely from each one of those encounters with the situation in the hands of the law was a tribute to him and to his courage, and of course to what must have been an inborn ability to cope with any given situation.

She squirmed back in her seat till her shoulders touched the padded back rest; she jerked the lines and made her horse lengthen his stride. When he moved out ahead of Canavan, the mare snorted and promptly bounded after the buggy horse, overtook him almost at once, and would have passed him if Canavan hadn't checked her and forced her to keep pace with Elena's horse. The frustrated mare fought for her head. But Canavan refused to yield and kept a firm grip on the reins. There was a brief spirited tussle, between horse and rider. But the mare, who had never mastered her master, was the one who surrendered. She grumbled a bit deep down in her throat, but the iron-handed Canavan ignored it. When she finally subsided and obeyed, he reached down and patted her and she whinnied happily.

Elena, who had watched the tussle with interest, smiled and said: "I guess she knows who's boss."

"Not always, though."

"Well, womanlike, she probably feels she has to kick up her heels every once in a while just to let you know she has a mind of her own. It doesn't mean that she expects you to give in to her. She just wants to . . . to try you out. I think she'd be disappointed if you yielded to her. The fact that you didn't renews her respect for you."

"Hope so."

She returned her attention to her own horse. But when she felt Canavan's eyes on her, she looked up and asked: "What is it, John? Why are looking at me like that?"

"Just thinking how lucky I am to have a wife like you."

"Thank you, but—"

"You know what we're in for. But because I don't want to cut and run, you're willing to go along with me on it. Not many women would take that attitude."

"Maybe it's because their husbands aren't John Canavans. That makes me luckier than they are by far. Oh, I get frightened and panicky just as they do. Don't think I don't. Fortunately you're the kind of man that you are. You're strong and determined, and when I lose heart and falter, you give me the strength I need to go on."

He smiled, and reached down and squeezed her shoulder.

"Oh, if I could only whinny . . ." she said.

They laughed together. Slowing herself, the mare turned her head and gave Canavan a questioning look, turned her head the other way, and eyed Elena obliquely and almost resentfully. It was only when Canavan jerked the reins that she finally squared around again. She grumbled a bit as she resumed her quick pace.

"I think her nose is out've joint, John," Elena said. "Somehow she knows we're both females, and you and I laughing together must be some form of intimacy that she resents. Pat her again to assure her that you love her too."

ELEVEN

It was the middle of the next morning when Stonebridge brought Ed Stoner, a slightly taller than average, wiry, iron-gray-haired man of about fifty or fifty-two, out to the JC to meet Canavan. Canavan suggested Bannon be there too. The meeting lasted little more than fifteen minutes, and resulted in the sale of Stoner's herd to Canavan, who also agreed to add the cattleman's three remaining hands to the JC crew.

"You'll find they're good men," Stoner assured Canavan. "No boozers. Just good, steady, reliable men who know their jobs and who'll give you a full day's work every day."

Canavan nodded and said: "I'm still in the market for more good beef stock and if you know—"

"That's what you're getting from me," Stoner said.

"Know anybody else 'round these parts who might have some that I can go after?"

Rubbing his nose with the back of his hand, Stoner gave a moment's frowning thought to the matter, finally shook his head and answered: "No-o, can't think of anybody right off. But if I do think of somebody you might go an' see, I'll get word to you."

"I'll be obliged to you," Canavan said. He turned to Bannon and said to him: "Think you and the boys you're taking with you had better get saddled up, Tom. You've got a long ride ahead of you so you might as well get started."

"Right," was Bannon's reply as he strode off.

Canavan walked with Stoner and Stonebridge to the latter's rig, and as the two men prepared to climb in, he followed Bannon, MacNaughton, Haber, and Jeffords into the corral.

"Tom," he said, and Bannon stopped and turned around.

"It's forty miles from Stoner's place back here. How long d'you figure it oughta take you to make it back?"

"Oh-h, don't think you oughta count on seeing us back here in less than a week. Figure those steers to do six to eight miles a day, and chances are it won't be any more than six. Yeah, figure it'll take us all of a week."

"Uh-huh. And if it takes a day or two longer, it'll still be all right. Don't want you to go pushin' that herd too hard or too far. If you do, you'll leave a trail of dead cattle all along the way."

Retracing his steps to the waiting buggy, Canavan stood talking with Stoner and Stonebridge till Bannon and the others rode up.

"You people go ahead," Bannon said to Stonebridge. "We'll catch up with you." Then after the buggy had rolled away, heading for downgrade, Bannon asked: "What about Dwyer and Sawyer?"

"What about them?"

"You're gonna find something for them to do, aren't you? They aren't used to sittin' around all day on their backsides."

"Oh, I'll keep them busy."

"What about those things you said you wanted to get from town? You know . . . hay, oats, salt. Oh, yeah . . . and mattresses for the three new men's bunks. How about sending Dwyer in the wagon into town to get the stuff?"

"I've gotta go to the bank to sign some kind o' paper for Stonebridge so's he can pay Stoner. So there wouldn't be any point sending Dwyer, being that I'll be there."

"No-o, suppose not."

"On top o' that, Thayer might hold back selling something to Dwyer. I don't think he will with me. Same time, being that we aren't too popular in Indian Head, if Dwyer was to go and some damned fool—"

"Y'mean, say, somebody like Had Voight or maybe Ab Peaseley?"

Canavan smiled and continued with: "If either of th'm, 'specially Had, was to find out that Dwyer rides for me, Had, even more than Peaseley, might take it into his head to pull something on Dwyer that he wouldn't try on me. No telling, y'know, what a harebrained character like Had might cook up. So I'll do the going to town whenever we need something. Be safer that way."

Then after Bannon and the three hands whom he had picked to help drive Stoner's herd southward to the JC had ridden away with him, Canavan, who had already spotted Dwyer and Sawyer sitting on the bunkhouse doorstep, sauntered down there. The two men looked up at him.

"Got something for us to do, boss?" the light-haired Phil Sawyer asked as he climbed to his feet.

Dwyer stood up too.

"I've gotta go into town to get some things," Canavan told them. "While I'm away, I'd like you two to do what you can getting things organized in the barn. Kinda messed up in there."

"Right," Sawyer said with a nod.

"The women are alone in the house," Canavan continued. "While I'm not expecting anybody to come snoopin' around, y'never know. So keep an eye out."

Again it was Sawyer who nodded and who said, as he had a moment before, "Right."

"Be a good feller, Dwyer, and hitch up the wagon for me."

"Sure, boss," Dwyer said, and strode off to the barn and disappeared inside.

For a moment or so there was silence between Canavan and Sawyer. Then Sawyer said: "Tom thought we oughta know what's been going on between you, the feller who runs the town, and that old feller he made sheriff. So he told us. Oh-h, and about that young squirt who's been doggin' you and taking potshots at you." When there was no comment from Canavan, Sawyer went on. "Now the way we see it, long's we sleep under your roof and in your bed, eat your grub and draw our pay from you, we owe you something more'n just doing our day's work for you. The way we pay back is, well, whatever kind o' grief you've got with somebody just naturally becomes our grief. What I mean is, if you've got trouble with anybody, so've we."

"Well, now—"

"Lemme finish, boss. I don't usu'lly go in for making speeches. So when I get started on one, I've gotta get it offa my chest."

Canavan grinned at him. "Go on. I'm listening," he said. "And I'm all ears."

"Mightn't it be a good idea for one of us to trail along with you whenever you hafta go to town? You know—just in case? None of us thinks he's a gun slinger or a real fast gun. But we're as handy with our guns as some who think they're fast, and a helluva lot better with th'm than most. So how about me ridin' in with you, like I said, just in case?"

"Thanks, Sawyer. Mighty decent of you to offer to lend a hand. But I don't think I need it. I don't look for anybody to start 'nything with me. They've found out I play rough and for keeps. So I think they'll steer clear o' me."

Sawyer shrugged and said: "All right, boss. Whatever you

105

say. Just thought I oughta let you know how we feel about things."

"Thanks for telling me. Means a lot to me to know that you fellers are ready to back my play. Maybe I'll be sorry I didn't take you up on your offer to ride in with me. If I am, the next time I have to go, I'll holler loud and clear for somebody to ride with me. That's a promise."

"Here y'are, boss! All set to roll!"

It was Dwyer calling from the foot of the ramp in front of the barn, and he was pointing to the wagon and to the team of horses that was idling in the wagon's traces. Canavan acknowledged with a wave of his hand and strode briskly across the trampled dirt to where Dwyer and the hitched-up team were waiting.

Dwyer handed him the reins, and flashing a grin, asked: "Want some comp'ny, boss?"

"Thanks, Dwyer. But not today. Maybe next time."

"Sure, boss."

Canavan climbed up, took his place on the wide seat, and released the handbrake. He drove down the incline, turned the team in the roadway, and headed for Indian Head.

In the thick, screening brush that paralleled the veranda, there were two low-bent men who had crept into the brush several hours before, undetected then and undetected now. One was Paulie Voight, the other Tommy Thayer. Both had discarded their arm slings in order to obtain fuller freedom of movement. Young Thayer, who had found crouching most uncomfortable, had taken to kneeling and alternately sinking down in the thinly grassed dirt on his backside, shifting himself and squirming about and muttering to himself, never still, never quiet. Finally, when his hardier and uncomplaining companion had endured it as long as he could, he twisted around, and in a low, guarded voice that was hardly more than a whisper, demanded of him: "Hell's the matter with you, Tommy? You so scared or you got the fidgets? And what's all that mumbling about?"

"My arm hurts," Tommy answered grumpily.

"Sh-h," Paulie cautioned him. "Keep your voice down." He peered out, drew back, and turned again to Thayer. "So your arm hurts, huh? Wanna know something? Mine does too, and what's more, so does my shoulder. But you don't hear me complaining, do you? You wanna know why you don't? Because I'm out here for a purpose, and I don't aim to let anything, not my arm or my shoulder or anything else, interfere with what I'm here to do."

Tommy Thayer was motionless for a change, and quiet.

106

"You make me wish it was Curly who was here with me instead o' you," Paulie continued. "He was no bellyacher. He was a man, every last inch of him."

"Yeah?" Tommy flung back at him. "And where's he now? And what did that being such a man get him? I'll tell you. A hole in the ground with worms to keep him company, and everybody sayin' what a damned fool he was."

Paulie Voight looked long and hard at him.

"Tommy, you really as hot to get square with that Canavan sonuvabitch as you want me to think you are?"

"I told you what I was doing yesterday, didn't I, doggin' him every which way and peggin' shots at him every time I came close enough? Does that sound like I don't aim to get hunk with him for cripplin' me?" Thayer countered.

"And I told you that that was stupid kid stuff, and that you were luckier than you have the right to be that he didn't go after you and gun you down. But that was yesterday, and yesterday's gone, so forget it. This is another day, and it's gonna be our day, the day we hit that redheaded bastid right where he lives, where it will hurt him more than anything that anybody could do to him."

"By takin' out on his wife what we've got against him? That doesn't make sense to me. What'd she ever do to us? He's the one who did it, and he's the one we shoulda gone after when he rode outta here."

"Oh-h, so we're back to that again, huh? Look, Tommy. We owe him something for what he did to us. Right? You tried to get square with him by doggin' him and peggin' shots at him. But nothing came of it. I'm not up to going after him. So what's the next best thing to do to hurt him? Hit him through his wife. Now, like I told you, old man Robbins' shack—you remember it, don't you, 'way up in the hills? That's where we're gonna take her. We'll leave a trail for Canavan to follow. Being that we'll have a good head start on him, we'll be all set up there, just holed in, you on one side and me on the other side, waiting for him. We'll let him come almost all the way up before we cut down on him."

"How long d'you figure we'll have to stay up there in the hills?" Tommy asked. "Gets awf'lly cold up there, y'know, 'specially at night."

"We mightn't have to stay up there at all. Depends on how soon after we've gone Canavan gets back and on how long it takes him to pick up the trail and follow us. And don't worry about the cold. I've got three good blankets, the best ones my mother's got, strapped on my saddle."

"Uh-huh. And what d'we do for grub if we have to stay put up there, say, for a day or two?"

Paulie grinned at his younger companion. "When we started out, you wanted to know what I had in my saddlebags that stuffed them out so. Remember? I told you you'd find out later on. Well, it's later on now. So I can tell you. Those saddlebags are full o' grub."

"Uh-huh," Thayer said again.

"Y'see, I don't go off half-cocked on anything. Everything I'm gonna do, I plan for. That way I don't forget anything. And I don't overlook anything. Now just to—to reassure you, Tommy, if you hadda killed Canavan yesterday, nobody woulda said a word about it. And if we have the luck to get him today, it'll be the same way. My old man's been trying every way he knows how to get rid of Canavan, and being that he runs the town and Ab Peaseley's the old man's sheriff, you oughta know damned well that nobody, 'specially the law, is gonna be after you, or me. When you get right down to it, by killing the bastid we'll be doing Indian Head a service."

"But what about her, Paulie? What about Canavan's wife?"

"What d'you mean, what about her?"

"Well, what we're fixin' to do to her, leastways that's what it amounts to the way I see it, is kidnap her. Right? Y'can swing for kidnapping a woman. Y'know that?"

Paulie frowned. "You're the damnedest scaredy-cat I've ever met up with," he said. "I'm just after telling you that you've got nothing to worry about, and you come back at me with something about kidnapping and that we c'n swing for it. You'll never know how much I meant it before when I said I wished it was Curly who was here with me instead o' you."

"You want me to go and—?"

"No, damn you! You know I can't pull this thing off by myself. If I had two good hands instead o' one, you wouldn't be here now. But I haven't, so I had to bring you in on this. Now get this, Tommy, and get it right. You've come this far with me, you're gonna see it through right down to the end. So you'd better make up your mind to that, or I'll fix you good. And you give me a hard time, I'll do it anyway."

Tommy held his tongue for about half a minute. Then he asked: "When are we gonna make our move?"

"Soon's I know what those two mavericks out there are gonna do," Paulie answered. "They went into the barn more'n five minutes ago. But they haven't come out yet. I'm hoping they're saddling up and that they're gonna go somewhere and leave us alone here so's we can do what we have to."

"Can I ask you something without you jumping all over me?"

Paulie grinned at Thayer, a little thinly though. " 'Course," he responded with an attempt at amiability that didn't quite come off. It was plain that he had to force himself to sound friendly because he needed Tommy. "Ask away, boy."

Thayer gave him a look that reflected his awareness that Paulie, whom he had always thought liked him, actually had little fondness for him and that he was tolerating him because he needed him.

"Yeah? What d'you wanna know?"

"Forget it."

"Aw, come on now, Tommy," Paulie coaxed him. "Don't be like that."

"I said forget it, didn't I?"

"You're takin' this all wrong, Tommy. We're friends. So that gives us the right to sound off at each other every once in a while. But that hasn't anything to do with our being friends. What were you gonna ask me?"

Thayer didn't answer. He moved past Paulie on his knees, parted the brush and stole a quick, guarded look outside, backed off again, and avoided Paulie's eyes.

"All right," the latter said with a lift of his shoulders. "If you wanna go on being sore . . ."

"Look," Tommy said curtly. "Like you said a while ago we're here for a purpose. When you're ready to make your move, just lemme know, tell me what you want me t'do, and I'll do it."

"But you still don't like the idea of what we're gonna do, do you?"

"Long's I'm willing to do it and go through with it, what difference does that make to you whether I like it or not?"

Paulie shrugged and said: "None, I don't suppose."

"Then we don't have to say 'ny more about it. Just do it."

"Uh-huh. Did you see anything, any sign o' those two hands when you took a peek outside?"

"Nope. No sign o' them or anybody else."

"We'll wait another couple o' minutes, just in case. Then we'll make our move," Paulie said. He reached beyond him and produced two good-sized gunnysacks; he handed one to his companion and retained the second one. "Now get this, Tommy, and get it right. Because once we're inside the house, we're gonna have to move fast, do our stuff, and get right out again."

"Uh-huh," Thayer said.

Low-voiced but even-toned, and with surprising patience, Paulie detailed his plan. Tommy listened attentively, without interrupting even once. Paulie finished briefing him, and said simply: "That's it."

"Uh-huh," Thayer said a second time.

"Got it?"

"Yeah, sure. Simple enough, so what's not to get?"

"Lemme have one last look outside. If the coast is clear, we'll make our move right now. We can't wait all day for those two lousy punchers. Who knows what they're doing down there in the barn?" Paulie peered out, and apparently satisfied, turned his head and hissed at Thayer: "All clear. Let's go."

There was activity in the street, marketing women and men passersby, proof that it wasn't as hot or oppressive as it had been the day before, Canavan noticed, when he wheeled the big, cumbersome farm wagon into Indian Head. He drove down the street, pulled up at the curb directly opposite the bank, pulled back hard on the handbrake, whipped the reins around it, and jumped down. He crossed the street and entered the bank.

Stonebridge, who was seated at his desk at the far rear thumbing through some papers, raised his eyes when he heard Canavan's step. As he got up, he said with a smile: "Didn't take you long to get here."

"No point delaying things," Canavan said as he came up to the desk. He thumbed his hat up from his forehead, and added: "Got some things we need from town. So I'm killing two birds with one stone. Those papers you want me to sign, they ready?"

"No, but it shouldn't take me more than a few minutes to prepare them for your signature."

"Look. Suppose while you're getting them ready, I go across the street to that Floyd Thayer's place, get what I've come for, and come back here, sign the papers and get going again? That way I won't be putting the rush on you and it'll be saving me time. All right?"

"Yes, of course."

Settling his hat more securely on his head, Canavan gave the banker a half salute, turned on his heel, and went striding out. Returning to the wagon, he climbed up and drove on down the street.

As he neared Ossie Blue's saloon, he recognized two men who were idling on the walk in front of the place. They were the two townsmen whom he had surprised and "captured" in Floyd Thayer's back yard and whom he had imprisoned in Thayer's cellar. Jess, the one whom he had manhandled, was the bigger of the two, and a burly individual. Recognizing Canavan, Jess glowered at him. His companion, Walt, simply lifted his eyes to Canavan, but showed no change of expression. Then as Canavan came abreast of them, Jess spat across

110

the walk, and said scornfully and loud enough for his words to carry, "Lousy sonuvabitch."

Canavan brought his team to an abrupt stop, braked the wagon, dropped the lines across the horses' backs, and swung down from the wide seat. Hitching up his belt, he crossed the walk. He stopped squarely in front of the two men, leveled his gaze at Jess, and asked: "What was that you said?"

Jess glared at him for a moment, then without answering, turned away. Moving after him, Canavan caught him by the arm, stopping him.

"I asked you something," Canavan said quietly. "I'm still waiting for you to answer me."

Jess looked down at the restraining hand that Canavan had clamped on his arm, and said gruffly: "Take your hand off me."

"All right," Canavan said, and removed his hand. "But the next time you go sonuvabitchin' me—"

"Yeah?" Jess taunted him.

"I'll knock your teeth down your throat."

Jess grinned evilly. "Oh, you will, huh?"

"That's right."

Their eyes met and clashed. Suddenly Jess spun around and swung mightily with his right. The punch was clumsily thrown, wildly too, and Canavan easily ducked under it and came up with one of his own, a short, hard left that he buried wrist-deep in the off-balance Jess's ample midsection. It brought a painful gasp from Jess, who instinctively folded his thick left arm over his stomach, yelled, "Grab him, Walt!" and aimed another blow at Canavan. Quickly backing away even though the punch was too short, Canavan half-turned so that he could keep both Jess and Walt in front of him, and feigned a swing at Walt, who hastily retreated. Pivoting, Canavan drove a pulverizing blow into Jess's unprotected face. It exploded with such force that Jess rocked under it and brought up both arms, the left a little lower than the right to protect his body, the right to ward off punches to the face and head. Blood gushed from his bashed-in nose and flaked his battered lips. Steadying himself, he rushed at Canavan, took a hard left to the face, and drove a straight right at Canavan. The latter, off balance for the moment, couldn't avoid it, but managed to ride with the blow, robbing it of its effectiveness. Jess's hard fist glanced off the side of Canavan's head, knocking his hat off. When it fluttered and fell almost at his feet, Canavan kicked it away. Apparently thinking that he had Canavan, Jess swarmed forward again, clubbing Canavan with his right and pawing at him with his left, only to have

111

the faster-of-hand-and-foot Canavan glide in, drumbeat half a dozen short-arm punches to the body, and back out again.

When Jess missed with a lunging right, Canavan's left landed squarely and closed Jess's left eye. But Jess continued to press forward, though not as recklessly as he had before. Circling around Canavan with his left outthrust and his balled-up right fist held high and in front of his blood-smeared face, he continued to stalk his opponent. Suddenly Canavan, moving with Jess, became aware of onlookers—men, women, even a couple of aproned shopkeepers—who were bunched together on the opposite walk, watching with wide eyes. He caught a glimpse too of Ossie Blue, wide-eyed and a little open-mouthed, standing just a step inside the saloon doorway. There were others surrounding Ossie, but they weren't familiar to Canavan, who ignored them.

"Come on, damn you!" Jess yelled at Canavan. "Come on and fight!"

Jess stopped his stalking and practically hurled himself at Canavan, who stood his ground. There was a flurry of punches, the thud of them landing, and Jess, who had gotten the worst of the exchange, began to retreat with his chest heaving, his mouth open as he sucked in air. Now it was Canavan who did the stalking and pursuing, landing solidly to the head and making Jess blink, then shifting his attack to the body, causing Jess to wince and give ground. Now Jess made little or no attempt to fight back, contenting himself with covering up as best he could as he continued to absorb Canavan's best punches. Apparently he was satisfied that he could weather the storm, that when Canavan had spent himself and had punched himself out, he would take command. A couple of times Canavan stopped and eyed him curiously, a sign that he was wondering what was keeping Jess upright. But each time Jess spat at him through his puffed and swollen lips, and cursed him too, and grimly Canavan went on battering him. Canavan stopped again when Jess rocked and swayed and even tottered. But instead of crumpling up, he managed somehow to steady himself, and he beckoned and rasped at Canavan: "C'mon, you lousy bastid! C'mon!"

Canavan needed no urging. He sank two hard, hooking lefts into Jess's belly that brought the latter's guard down. Instantly a long, swishing, thunderous right that carried the full weight of Canavan's supple body in its grasp crashed against Jess's jaw and his legs buckled under him and he fell in a heap. The fight was over.

A couple of townsmen who came across the street helped Walt get Jess up on his feet and they led him away. Canavan picked up his hat and beat it against his leg, ridding it of the dust that it had acquired slithering about on the walk. He clapped it on his head, tucked in his shirttail, and returned to the wagon. Pretending to be unaware of the eyes that were holding on him and following him, he drove on to the Emporium.

Floyd Thayer was standing on the walk in front of his place when Canavan braked the wagon to a stop at the curb. Thayer glanced at him, then turned and tramped back inside. He was standing behind the counter when Canavan entered. Floyd lifted his gaze and held it on him as he crossed the floor to the counter.

"I need a couple o' things," Canavan said.

"Like what?"

Canavan smiled a little and answered: "Like three more bunk mattresses. Oh-h, how about those branding irons? When'll they be ready?"

"They're ready now," was the reply. "Fact is, they've been ready and waiting for you since last night."

Canavan nodded and asked: "How about hay and feed and salt? I get th'm from you or do I—"

"You c'n get them at the stable."

"Oh," Canavan said. "Wanna get those mattresses for me now like a good feller? Oh, and the irons too."

Thayer grunted and when he emerged from behind the counter at the far end, Canavan followed him. Minutes later they returned, with Thayer carrying one of the mattresses and Canavan the other two. The mattresses were upended in the wagon and leaned against the sides.

When Canavan turned, Thayer handed him a paper-wrapped package. "The irons," the storekeeper said.

Canavan dropped the package in the wagon. Then he followed Thayer back into the store, and waited while Thayer prepared a bill and laid it before him on the counter. Canavan looked at it, nodded, took the stub of a pencil that the storekeeper held out to him, scribbled "J. Canavan" at the bottom of it, handed it back together with the pencil, and went out.

He stood for a moment or so on the walk, looking up the street, then came around the idling team and stepped down into the gutter. He had no particular reason for doing that since he could easily have climbed up into the wagon from the curb side instead of mounting to the driver's seat from the gutter side.

A rifle cracked ominously and spitefully and his hat was torn off his head and sent fluttering away. Instinctively he replied to the rifle shot. For a long moment he stood motionlessly, his hard eyes fixed on the alleyway directly opposite the

113

Emporium, for it was from there that the shot had been fired at him. And it was just inside the alley, actually in the entrance to it, that he had glimpsed the rifleman at the very moment that he had leaned out and fired. Now there was no sign of him. Men came running from every direction. But they skidded to an abrupt stop when they saw Canavan, gun in hand and half-raised for a quick shot, slowly cross the street over which a deathly silence had suddenly draped itself.

When he stepped up on the curb and halted in the middle of the walk, he stared hard at the hunched-over body that lay in the alley against the side of one of the buildings that walled it in. It wasn't the flat-bellied body of Tommy Thayer as he had expected it to be. It was instead the potbellied body of a big, burly, beefy man. The man named Jess.

TWELVE

The big wagon, with its broad-tracked iron-rimmed wheels biting deep into the dirt behind the team of straining horses, forged its way up the incline, topped it, rumbled on toward the barn, and halted at the foot of the ramp. Phil Sawyer appeared in the open doorway.

"Oh," he said when he saw Canavan.

"Everything all right here?" the latter asked as he whipped the reins around the drawn-back handbrake.

"Yeah, sure," was Sawyer's reply as he started down the ramp. When he saw the mattresses and the bales of hay, he turned his head and called: "Hey, Lee! C'mon down here and gimme a hand!"

"With what?" Dwyer wanted to know, poking his head out.

He hitched up his levis and came down the ramp to Sawyer's side. He stepped around him to the rear of the wagon, unhooked the tailgate, and let it drop. As he hauled himself up into it, Canavan climed down from the driver's seat.

"How'd things go in town, boss?" Dwyer heard Sawyer ask. "Peaceable for a change?"

Canavan balled up his fists and held them up so that Sawyer could see the skinned knuckles.

The latter peered at them and said: "H'm. From the looks o' th'm, I'd say you musta done a helluva job on somebody." Then raising his eyes to Canavan's face, he added: "Kinda red under the eyes. Outside o' that, though, you look all right. More like you've been to prayer meeting than in a fight."

Canavan grunted, turned, and headed for the house. Sawyer and Dwyer followed him with their eyes as he trudged up the path that ran parallel to the side veranda and led to the rear of the house. As he rounded it and disappeared, Dwyer said: "Don't think I'd wanna hook up with him in a knock-down and dragout fight."

"Don't think I would either."

"Got the biggest pair o' hands I ever saw and shoulders to match. Wide as a gate. I'll bet the feller he hauled off on will have a headache for a month. Wonder what he looked like when Canavan got finished with him."

"Probably like he'd tangled with a mountain lion."

"Or like he'd got himself caught in a stampede and was trampled on. Oh, these mattresses go into the bunkhouse, don't they?"

" 'Course. They're for the three new hands who'll be coming back with Bannon."

As Dwyer prepared to push the first mattress over the side of the wagon and lower it into Sawyer's hands, there was a rush of booted feet in the path, and the two men looked wonderingly in its direction. As they held their gaze on it, Canavan burst into view and came dashing down to the barn. He skidded to a stop just short of the idling team of horses. One of them looked up at him, the other did not, in fact showed no interest in him whatsoever.

Canavan was grim-faced, his eyes steely, his chest heaving. "One o' you saddle up for me and hustle it," he panted. "My wife's gone. Two men slipped into the house from the back, jumped Maria, threw a gunnysack over her, tied her up, and dumped her into a closet and slammed the door shut on 'er."

Dwyer stared at him.

"Then they went upstairs, musta done the same thing to Elena, that is, threw a sack over her too, probably after gagging her," Canavan continued, "and got out the back door with her."

"Holy cow," Sawyer said. "And we didn't hear a damned thing down here."

Dwyer didn't wait to hear any more. He jumped down from the wagon, lost his balance and landed in the dirt on his backside, cursed and scrambled to his feet, and scampered up the ramp and disappeared inside the barn.

"I'll saddle up too, boss," Sawyer said, "and go with you."

"No. You fellers stay here. Maria's in a bad way. You two go up to the house and stay there with her. Don't want her left alone."

Sawyer looked disappointed.

"Need two of us for that?" he asked. "Won't Lee be enough? What can happen to her now? It doesn't figure

116

that those two highbinders, whoever they are, who got away with your missus are gonna come back again, does it?"

"No-o, I suppose not. All right, Sawyer. Get saddled up."

"Right," Sawyer said alertly and started up the ramp. Then he stopped and looked back at Canavan, who was pacing about, grinding his big right fist into the palm of his left hand. "Boss . . ."

Canavan's pacing halted abruptly. He looked up at Sawyer.

"Got 'ny idea which way they mighta gone from here?"

"Same direction they came from," Canavan answered, and he pointed beyond the house.

"And who they mighta been?"

"All I know is what Maria said, that they were young fellers. She got a look at them, but everything happened so fast, I don't think she'd know them if she ever saw th'm again."

"Young fellers, huh?" Sawyer repeated thoughtfully. "Hey, think one o' th'm coulda been that kid who's been doggin' you and takin' potshots at you?"

"I thought o' that. Yeah, he coulda been one o' th'm."

Sawyer wheeled around and ran up the ramp. Minutes later Lee Dwyer reappeared, leading the mare. He brought her down to Canavan and handed him the reins.

"She sure is leery of strangers, isn't she?" Dwyer asked as Canavan swung himself up on the mare's back. "For a minute there I was afraid she was gonna kick my head off. Had to sweet-talk her before she'd let me get close enough to slap her saddle on 'er." When there was no response from Canavan, who sat tight-lipped and hard-eyed with his gaze fixed on the barn doorway, Dwyer went on: "Wish I was going with you and Phil, boss. I'd sure like to be in on it when you catch up with those two polecats. Hell of a way to get square with a man by hittin' him through his wife. For my dough—"

"What's taking him so long?" Canavan asked impatiently, interrupting Dwyer.

Before the latter could answer, hoofs thumped hollowly on the barn floor, and Sawyer rode out astride his horse.

"All set, boss," he announced as he came off the ramp.

"Dwyer," Canavan said, and Dwyer looked at him. "Hustle yourself up to the house and stay put there with Maria. I don't want her left alone, not even for a minute. Understand?"

"Yeah, sure," was the reply and Dwyer headed for the house on the run.

"Let's go," Canavan said to the waiting Sawyer.

With Canavan leading the way and holding the prancing, eager-to-be-off-and-running mare down to a trot, and with

117

Sawyer diagonally behind them, they went up the path, glimpsed Dwyer as he rounded the house, loped past it, rode through the grove of cottonwoods beyond it, and shortly broke into the open. They pulled up while Canavan ranged a quick look about them. He shook his head and said: "Figures those two who got away with Elena must have some out-a-the-way place all set up for them to hole up in. But being that I don't know much about the countryside around here, I'm kinda stumped. Dunno which way to turn or where to go looking."

"We could sure use Bannon and the others right now, couldn't we?"

"And how we could! Going off by ourselves, we c'n go chasing our tails around the whole county without finding them. All I know is that I'll keep after th'm no matter how long it takes, and when I do catch up with th'm . . ."

Sawyer loped away from him, snatched something off a thinly branched, scrawny bush, and wheeled around with it. He held it up for Canavan to see. Canavan came drumming up to him and eyed it, a torn-off piece of white cloth.

"Think this could mean something, boss?" Sawyer asked him.

"Looks like a peice o' kitchen towel," Canavan answered. "Think it's the kind that Maria uses."

Sawyer twisted around in the saddle.

"There's another piece," he said, and pointed.

Together the two men headed for it. This time it was Canavan rather than Sawyer who retrieved it.

"Same kind's the other piece," Sawyer said.

"Yeah," Canavan said, comparing the two. "If we find any more . . ."

"You thinking the same thing I'm thinking?"

"Like I started to say, if we find any more o' these pieces, I'll know for sure."

"Y'mean that they've marked the trail that they took to make it easy for you to follow them?"

"Uh-huh," Canavan said, clutching the two pieces of cloth in his left hand, suddenly balling them up into a small, tight mass and stuffing it into his pants pocket. "Looks to me like they want me to follow th'm right to where they'll be set and waiting for me to ride into whatever kind o' trap they've got rigged up so they can catch me between them and gun me down."

"And they grabbed your missus to bait the trap with, right?"

"Can't figure it any other way."

"Then it's a good thing there are two of us. When we come

118

to where they're waiting for you to show up, we can separate and each of us take on one o' them. That oughta do something to kinda spoil what they've got set up."

"Yeah, guess it will."

They spied a third piece of cloth impaled on a bush shortly after that. Wheeling their horses, they hurried to snatch up still another piece that lay limply on the grass with the open road just below and beyond the spot. They guided their mounts down the slight embankment that led to the road. At the same instant the two men spotted a fifth piece that was caught on a bent nail in the side of a sagging wooden fence post on the opposite side of the road.

Just as they were about to cross the road, they heard oncoming hoofbeats, and Sawyer, turning to Canavan, asked: "You don't suppose that could be them, do you, boss?"

Canavan shook his head. "No, don't think so," he replied. "But we'll wait and see."

Quietly and motionlessly, then, they sat their horses and waited for the horsemen to come into view. They did shortly and as they came steadily closer, Canavan said: "They aren't the ones we're after."

"Oh?"

"They're the Voights."

"The who? Oh-h, yeah! The characters who've been giving you such a hard time, right?"

"One o' th'm has."

"Boss, y'think he mighta had something to do with this? Y'know, like putting those two young mavericks up to runnin' off with Elena—your missus?"

"No," Canavan said flatly. "I know he wants to get rid o' me in the worst way. But I don't think he's the kind who'd go in for kidnapping."

"Uh-huh," Sawyer said. "One o' those Voights has his arm in a sling. He the one who's been giving you trouble?"

"No," Canavan replied with a shake of his head. "That one's Al. And he isn't a bad sort. It's the other one, Had, who's the troublemaker."

"He doesn't look like much from here. Kinda skinny, I'd say, and maybe a mite puny."

"When you get a better look at him, you'll see that he isn't either one. He's about average in size and build. The trouble with him is that he thinks who the hell he is, and he's got a bad temper. Combination of the two is what gets him into trouble."

The Voights came drumming up presently. When Al saw Canavan, he said something side-mouthed to Had, and the two reined in, Had a little reluctantly, it seemed to Canavan.

Had's expression mirrored the fact that he was not overly happy at the prospect of coming face-to-face with Canavan. So while Al eased back a bit in the saddle, the elbow of his broken arm cradled in the palm of his left hand, his calm eyes on Canavan, Had stared sullenly at the ground.

Canavan knee-nudged the mare into movement and brought her up alongside of Al's horse.

"You look kinda mad," Al said. "S'matter? Somebody step on your corns?"

"I've got plenty to be mad about," Canavan replied. "Two young squirts broke into my house while I was in town, roughed up the Mexican woman who works for us, and made off with my wife."

Al gave him an odd, oblique look. Had's head came up with a sudden jerk, and he stared hard at Canavan, almost unbelievingly.

"They spotted these things around for me to follow," Canavan continued, and hauled out the balled-up pieces of cloth so that the two Voights could see them. When he pointed to the piece that still hung from the fence post, their eyes followed his pointing finger. "I kinda think that Thayer kid was one o' th'm."

"If you think we had anything to do with your wife's kidnapping," Had said heatedly, "you couldn't be more wrong."

"I don't think you did," Canavan answered calmly. "So keep your shirt on."

"That damned Tommy Thayer," Al said. "Think I told you, Canavan, when I ran into you and your wife, that that kid's a bad one, and that sure as shootin' he'll wind up at the end of a rope, 'less you kill him first. Now who the other kid could be, I don't know for sure, so I won't try to guess."

"You don't have to," Canavan told him curtly. "I knew who he was right from the start, because it figured it had to be him. That first day in Indian Head for me when I went into Ossie Blue's saloon for a beer, there were three o' them at the bar, kinda playful they were too, and they tried to sucker me into payin' for beer for them. No point in telling you what happened. You know same's I do. There was that Curly Simmons, the Thayer boy, and that kid o' yours, Had."

Had glared at him. "And you think Paulie was Tommy Thayer's accomplice in your wife's kidnapping," he said and his face began to redden.

"It figures," Canavan said simply.

Had was livid now. "How dare you accuse my son of participating in a crime when you don't know the facts?" he fairly yelled at Canavan.

120

"I'm not accusing him yet," Canavan retorted. "All I've said so far is that it figures that it's him who's in on this with young Thayer."

"I can name you a dozen others of about Paulie's age with whom he has been friendly," Had continued angrily, "and for your information, mister, any one of them could have—"

"A dozen, Had?" Al asked him.

Had whirled around at him. "Yes!" he snapped. "And maybe even more than just a dozen. Manly Voight's four sons, Judd Voight's, Andy Thayer's, Russell Thayer's, Lud Thayer's . . ."

"Had," Al said patiently. "There isn't a one o' those you've just mentioned still around Indian Head. Fact is, hasn't been for a couple o' years now. You wouldn't know, Had," and now his tone was even gentler, "because you never showed 'ny interest in people or in what went on with th'm. Only time you knew them was when you needed them or wanted something of th'm."

"Look, I'm wasting time here," Canavan said to Al. "Where will I wind up if I keep following this piéce o' rag trail? There any place up that way"— ͢͢d he indicated with a nod the opposite side of the road and the land that stretched away from the top of the embankment and lost itself in the distance—"where they can hole up?"

"That's Orvie Thayer's place over there," Al answered. "Tommy's grandpa. Couple o' miles from here, you'll run into some rough, rugged, hilly country. Hey, Had . . ."

Had was still smoldering. Despite it, he turned his head and looked questioningly, a little angrily too, at his brother.

"When Paulie was a kid," Al said, "didn't he used to like to go off somewhere's all by himself every once in a while, and once when he'd been gone for a whole day, and night was coming on, didn't we go looking for him and—?"

"We tracked him up into the hills and found him in an old shack," Had said.

"That's right," Al said. "Used to be an old feller named Robbins who lived there. He did some hunting an' trapping. Just enough to keep himself alive. Anyway, that's the only place I can think of, and if Paulie's mixed up in this kidnapping business, I'll betcha that's where they're holed up."

"Depend upon it," Had said doggedly, "Paulie's much too smart to let himself get involved in anything like this . . . this kidnapping. So you won't find him there. Where you will find him, I assure you, will be at his mother's place in town."

Neither Al nor Canavan made any response to that. Canavan settled himself in the saddle, glanced over his shoulder at the waiting Sawyer, who had kept his distance and who had made no attempt to inject himself into the give-and-take discussion, and said to him: "Let's go."

"I'll go along with you," Al said.

"I will, too," Had said, "so I can be on hand to accept your apology."

"If there's any apology coming to you, you'll get it even if you aren't there," Canavan told him. "So there's no call for you to trail along. That goes for you too, Al. Chances are there'll be some gunplay, and you know what happens to the innocent bystander when there's a shooting. He's the one who usu'lly gets shot. So you fellers go on where you were going and we'll go on same's we were when we met up with you. C'mon, Sawyer."

"I said I'd go along with you," Had said rather stiffly, "and that's what I intend to do."

"Al," Canavan said, turning to him. "You feel up to riding through rough country and gettin' yourself jarred and jounced around?"

"Let's go," Al said to his brother, completely ignoring Canavan's question.

"Couple o' stubborn old mules," Canavan muttered, and backed the mare away as Al wheeled his mount to Had's side.

With the Voights leading the way and Canavan and Sawyer moving into position behind them and topping the embankment after them, the four drummed over Orvie Thayer's property at a pretty fair pace. There was no conversation. Everyone seemed to be too thoroughly occupied with his own thoughts to indulge in any talk. A couple of times the mare, unaccustomed to running in any kind of formation and unwilling to take anyone else's dust in her face, voiced a protest. She snorted and sought to pull up alongside of Al Voight to avoid the dust that his horse was kicking up. But Canavan held her back. She snorted even louder than before, grumbled, and then began to prance and run sideways. When he had had enough of it, he whacked her on the rump, and she ran straight although she continued to grumble. The miles fell away behind them under the swift pace that they were maintaining. Soon Canavan glimpsed the sketchy outline of some low-lying hills ahead of them in the distance. As they continued to narrow the distance, the outline grew steadily stronger until the full contour of the hills stood out quite plainly against the sky.

When Al slowed his horse to a trot, the others did too. Quite suddenly Canavan noticed that the grass that had carpeted the ground was gone, and that barren, shale-and-stone-strewn surfacing had replaced it. The beat of the horses' ironshod hoofs lifted and echoed as they clattered over it.

Now too he noticed that the land was lifting in a steady upgrade. A couple of times when he leaned down from the saddle, he spotted freshly cut hoofprints in the dirt. Sensing that Al had noticed them too even though he had made no mention of it, Canavan held his tongue.

Finally Al half-turned to him and asked: "Y'see those boulders and rock piles up ahead, say, oh-h, half a mile or so from here? And no cover of any kind, not even a tree stump, on any side leading up to it?"

"Uh-huh," Canavan said, hand-shading his eyes as he focused his gaze upon the indicated spot. "Where's the shack?"

"Those rocks an' boulders form a kind o' half circle, a kind o' cockeyed one, though, stretching right out from the hills. In the middle of the half circle is a clearing, and in the middle of the clearing is the shack. Get the picture?"

"Yeah, sure. Far as I can see this is the only trail up. That right?"

"Yep. This is the only one."

"And anyone coming up this way, like they're expecting me to do, would be right smack in the sights of a rifle, wouldn't he?"

Al nodded.

"Then you know damned well I won't follow this one up. I'll have to make it up there some other way. Maybe cut wide away from here to throw them off, and when I figure they've lost sight o' me, cut into the hills and work my way through th'm till I come up behind the shack and them."

All four had halted and now they stood together in a tight little bunch turned to each other.

"I don't think anyone's up there," Had Voight said.

"That's where you're wrong," Canavan said evenly. "They're up there all right. There were fresh hoofprints leading up this way starting back where the grass ended."

"He's right, Had," Al said. "I saw th'm too. So you can bet on it that they're up there, and chances are they're watching us and wondering how come there are four of us when they were only expecting Canavan. From where they are they can't make us out. They know that one of us has to be Canavan. But who the rest of us are must have them wondering and worrying."

"Tell you what," Canavan said, and all eyes held on him. "Let's all of us turn right around and go back down the way we came up. Then—"

"Yeah?" Al pressed him. "And then?"

"Like I said before, I'll swing wide from down below, find a spot to cut into the hills, and come up behind them."

"How about me doing the same thing, boss, from the other

side, to draw their fire and their . . . their attention away from you?" Sawyer asked.

"No," Canavan replied. "Once I come up behind them, that will be it. I won't need 'ny help then. So you and Al and Had'll stay put at the bottom of the trail and wait there for me. Now don't get me wrong, Sawyer. Don't think I don't appreciate your offering to trail along with me and lend a hand in whatever might come up. Believe me, I do. But from here on I'd rather go through with this on my own and not take any chances on you or anybody else stopping a slug when there isn't any call for it. Understand?"

Once again Sawyer looked disappointed. But before he could protest, Had said: "Before any of you does anything, I want the chance to prove to you that you've misjudged my son. Oh, I'm willing to believe that since both you, Canavan, and Al saw fresh tracks leading up this way, there are people up behind those boulders. But I know that Paulie isn't one of them. As his father, I have the right to demand a chance to prove it to you."

"And how d'you aim to do that?" Canavan asked him.

Had faced him squarely and met his eyes. "Only one way," he said quietly. "I'll go straight up there. Whoever it is up there must know me and won't dare do anything to stop me. So don't be too concerned for my safety."

"I don't like the idea," Canavan said flatly. "Fact is, I think it's a lousy idea, like most of the others you've come up with. Suppose before they recognize you, once they see you coming up at them, they start shooting? Then where'll you be? Out in the open without any cover and without any kind o' chance. Tell you what, Had. Being that I don't know for sure that Paulie is up there, I'm willing to go along with you and take your word for it that he isn't in on this thing and that he isn't up there either. He's your son, so you oughta know better'n anybody else what he—"

"I don't want any favors of you," Had said heatedly, interrupting him.

He wheeled away so suddenly that even though Canavan instinctively put out his hand in an effort to stop him, he failed to reach him and Had, whacking his horse with his open hand, an explosive, echoing slap, sent him scrambling up the trail.

When Canavan sought to go after him, Al moved squarely in front of him, blocking him, and said: "Let him go. Long's he feels that this is something he's gotta do, he's got the right to do it, and nobody has the right to stop him."

"They'll kill him," Canavan answered angrily. "You know same's he does and same's I do that Paulie hates his guts. He's

124

proved that, hasn't he? So what makes you think he'll hold his fire when he sees Had coming up there? All Paulie will think is that Had's gone out of his way to spoil his little game. So he'll cut down on Had same's he would on me. You're a pair o' pigheaded damned fools, you two. Instead o' stopping me from going after Had and stopping him from getting himself killed—"

Canavan didn't finish his angry tirade. When he saw an unrecognizable figure emerge from between two huge, white-faced boulders, and saw sunlight glint for an instant on the barrel of the man's half-raised gun, he jerked the reins and drove the mare squarely at Al's horse, trampling him, making him cry out, and forcing him to back off. Then the mare went scurrying up the trail.

"Go 'head, boss!" Sawyer yelled as he followed Canavan. "I'll cover you!"

"Hold it right there, Pop!" a voice that Canavan knew at once was Paulie Voight's yelled. "Don't come any closer! Now what are you doing here, and what d'you want?"

"I want to talk to you, Paulie," Had replied.

"You haven't got anything to say to me that I wanna hear!" Paulie yelled back at his oncoming father. "So turn yourself around and get outta here!"

When Had continued to press up the trail, there was another yell from Paulie: "You old fool! I told you to get outta here, didn't I?"

This time there was no answer from Had. Paulie's gun leveled and roared, and Had's horse cried out when the bullet, plowing into the dirt, flung it at him with stinging, painful force. Canavan, overtaking Had and coming up diagonally behind him, heard him gasp when Paulie fired a second time. The mare bounded past Had and Canavan snapped a shot at Paulie, pegged a second lightning shot at him when the youth backed against one of the boulders, and followed it with a third shot. Paulie sank back, impaled upon the boulder. He dropped his gun, slid down, and crumpled up in a hunched-over heap.

A second figure, Tommy Thayer, with his upraised gun in his hand, suddenly burst out from behind a pile of rocks, flung a shot at Canavan, and started to run off. There was a yell from Sawyer as he swerved away in pursuit of the youth. Tommy skidded to a stop, wheeled around, and fired at Sawyer as the latter came swooping down upon him and emptied his gun into him.

Pulling up close by the spot where Paulie Voight lay, Canavan flung himself off the mare, and holstering his gun, squeezed in between two boulders and disappeared. Minutes

125

later when he reappeared, he was carrying Elena in his arms and she had curled her arms around his neck and was clinging to him.

Sawyer rode up, and slacked a little in the saddle. "Missus all right, boss?" he asked.

"Yeah, she's fine now."

"Swell. Reckon, then, we can go home, huh?"

Canavan did not answer. When he saw Al Voight kneeling over Had, who lay on his back across the trail, he turned with Elena and carried her over to where the mare, having blown herself, stood waiting.

"Honey," he said. "Had's been shot. Think you'll be all right if I leave you here for a minute while I go see how bad he's been hit?"

"Of course, darling."

He kissed her and gently stood her up on her feet. The mare turned her head and whinnied and nuzzled Elena and she patted her.

Canavan joined Al at Had's side. Had's eyes were closed.

"Don't hold it against the boy, Al," he heard Had say faintly. "He didn't mean to hit me. He didn't really hate me as people thought he did."

" 'Course he didn't," Al assured him.

Had's shirt front was bloodstained, and more blood was seeping out of him and puddling the dirt under him. A sigh came from him, from deep down inside of him, and his body seemed to relax and sink a little deeper into the now brownish dirt.

"He's dead," Al said heavily as he got up on his feet.

"It took guts to do what he did," Canavan said.

Al nodded and asked: "Your wife all right?"

"Yeah," Canavan answered simply.

"I'd like to take Had home," Al said.

" 'Course."

It was Sawyer who produced a rope and who helped Canavan drape Had's body over the back of his horse and lash it on. The horses that had belonged to young Thayer and Paulie Voight were found behind the shack and the bodies of the two youths were slung over the animals' backs and tied on. Then, with Al mounted and leading the way, Elena up in front of Canavan on the mare, Sawyer following them, and the horses with the lashed-on bodies bringing up the rear, the party made its way down the grassless incline. When Canavan half-turned and beckoned, Sawyer pulled alongside of him.

"Like you to trail along with Al," Canavan told him low-voiced, "just to make sure he gets Had home all right."

Sawyer nodded and asked: "What about the other two?"

"One o' Had's hands can take them into town. So soon's you leave Al, you come on home."

"Right," Sawyer said. He halted his mount and moved into position again behind Canavan.

Later when they stopped in the roadway, Al turned to Elena and said gravely to her: "Glad you're all right, ma'am."

"Elena," she said.

"Elena," he repeated.

"When will you be burying Had?" Canavan asked.

"Tomorrow. Probably around the middle of the morning."

"I'll be there."

"So will I, Al," Elena said.

He looked both surprised and pleased and said: "I'll be obliged to both of you if you c'n make it."

"We'll make it," Elena and Canavan said together.

Apparently Al had overheard Canavan's instructions to Sawyer. He touched his hat to Elena, gave Sawyer a nod, and rode away. Herding the three horses with the lashed-on bodies ahead of him, Sawyer followed Al.

More SIGNET Westerns